A
KILLING
KINDNESS

Barbara Treat Williams

Spinsters Ink
2009

Attitude Books
P.O. Box 242
Midway, Florida 32343

Printed in the United States of America on acid-free paper
First Edition

Editor: Katherine V. Forrest
Cover designer: Linda Callaghan

ISBN: 10-1935226-04-5

ISBN: 13-978-1-935226-04-8

To the Lakota of Pine Ridge Reservation; and to Tom, Leslie and Jen—my co-travelers of Earth this time around.

Acknowledgment

I'd like to acknowledge Katherine V. Forrest for kindly showing me how to quilt my patchwork manuscript together. I'd also like to thank Little Sparrow, Two Doves and Adrianna, my guide, for their encouragement and friendship on the dark days. And, lastly, thanks to my tour guides and dear friends, Linda Badiuk and Dana Parks of Rapid City, South Dakota. I owe you all so much.

Chapter One

"Is she leaving that hunk?" A lady with brassy hair and big boobs elbowed me aside as I stood in the supermarket checkout line.

I felt cheated. After all, this was my time to chill. Like some people meditate or pray to go to that calm place, I look at the tabloids in the checkout line on my weekly supply jaunt into Clear Creek, Kansas. Will Kirsten lose weight? Are Brad and Angelina collaborating with extraterrestrials to adopt an alien child? Can Christ's image be found in a dark stain on a potato? I'm an eighteen-year-old woman who needs to find peace where I can and those few moments I wait and stare at those story lines in Al's Sav-A-Lot while the checkout guy scans my order usually do the trick. But, not today.

The woman pulled a magazine from the rack with fuchsia talons. "Too bad," she said. "Well, you know what they say. It takes two to tango." She gave me a bob of her head as if to emphasize the truth of it.

I've never agreed with that saying. Nice people hook up with jerks all the time, and it's usually the jerk's fault if things go south. I've seen it happen too many times to know it's not true.

Take, for instance, my Cousin Blair's recent attempt to manipulate me into going back to Pell Mell, South Dakota. I know there's something devious behind this invitation, and I don't much want to listen to her tell me what it is. Because Blair has a talent for somehow getting me involved in things that she creates but for which I get the blame. She'd called the shelter five times since yesterday, something about coming back to attend her father's wedding. Mickey had taken messages. The one time she did get through to me, she didn't have me at hello. I hung up. Colin hasn't given me the time of day since I was a kid, so I doubt he'd invite me to his wedding. I sense her motives are deeper. Meaner. She knows my mother was murdered there. I'd rather poke my eyes out than see that place again.

I hauled the groceries for the shelter through the rain to Aunt Angela's old pickup in a cart with a weird wheel that fought me all the way, pulling to the right and affecting my mood for the worse. Once I'd loaded the groceries and covered them with a tarp, I settled myself on the old plaid blanket that covered the hole in the front seat and adjusted the rearview mirror. I got a good look at the annoyance other people must be seeing in my brown eyes.

Aunt Angela has accused me of looking chronically pissed, so I made an effort to relax the tiny lines I saw. When I turned the key and the old blue Ford started right up, it went a long way toward getting my humor back. It grunted and farted all the way to the shelter, but it got me home and that was not always a given. I hit the kitchen door, arms full of the last sack, just in time to hear to the phone ring. I sat the sack down and picked up the old white Princess phone receiver.

"Can you talk?" Blair's voice came over the phone in a whisper as if spies were everywhere. Whenever I hear her breathy, little-girl voice, my stomach does a rinse cycle and spin. It's hard for me to be friendly to her when she's the biggest fan of one Billy Chance, a low-life cretin who has effed up my life like sugar in a gas tank. Did I mention he's the one who killed my mother?

"I mean, if it's convenient," she continued. "I can call back, yet again, if I have to."

"Do that," I said, and hung up.

I pictured her banging her cell phone against the wall in frustration and smiled. I'd like to say I pictured her with frizzy hair and braces. I'd really like to say that. But, no. When I last saw Blair, dressed in strategically ripped jeans that cost mucho bucks, her big brown eyes were flecked with little gold lights and her mahogany hair, well, tumbled to the middle of her back. She had pouted lips from Mother Nature, not a doctor. Her skin was porcelain. I'm sure a pimple would explode itself before it ever thought of lighting on her perfect nose.

"Was that Blair again?" Aunt Angela asked as she entered her spacious but dilapidated country kitchen. She stuck her hand in a plastic grocery bag and pulled out a couple boxes of mac and cheese and carried them to the cupboard. Her short haircut fell against her cheeks in little gray wisps, giving her the look of a middle-aged pixie. She had on faded jeans, loafers and a red gingham cowboy shirt the exact same print as the kitchen curtains. I guessed she'd scored another sale on bolts of cloth or an old bedspread at a garage sale somewhere and given them to Mickey to sew. Aunt Angela could stretch a buck further than Gumby. "You're going to have to take her call eventually," she said, "or we're never going to get any G D peace around here. Make it clear to her there's no way we're going to that wedding. Too many bad memories for both of us there."

Aunt Angela is a grown woman who finds it hard to curse. Her sentences are peppered with initials, and H E double hockey sticks, and other euphemisms. Because of her squeamishness, I try to keep the throttle down on my mouth, too. But right now I really wanted to say, "Screw Blair."

We continued to put the groceries away in companionable silence. I paced from the cans cabinet to the bread drawer to the fridge, and I again felt that wonderful sense of belonging I'd had since I came to live at St. Mary's three years ago. For some crazy reason, I love the peeling wallpaper and broken linoleum and the décor by Salvation Army. Maybe because it's the only real home I've had since Mom died. I stopped to straighten a framed picture of an angel watching little kids go over a rickety bridge.

"You think you'd be up to painting the outside this summer?" asked Aunt Angela as she unloaded a twelve pack of soda pop into the fridge. "Paint's on sale at Wal-Mart."

"Sure," I said, knowing it would be a big job for one person. But the white paint had gone to gray and the wraparound porch would look better with a new coat. We were so isolated, surrounded by wheat fields, that I thought it hardly made any difference what the place looked like. But, if she wanted it painted, I'd paint it. Besides, I liked working outside. St. Mary's squats on a slight rise in the land that affords me a good view of the pasture of the neighboring farms where wooly buffalo and snooty looking llamas tend their babies. It would be downright peaceful if it weren't for the handful of kids that were currently living in the house. Then again, it wouldn't be as much fun without those kids running around, either.

In what Aunt Angela calls the great room off the kitchen, I could hear Mickey welcoming a new girl to the house. I peeked around the corner to have a look. Mickey, with her frizzy red hair, gangly body and round blue eyes, looked for all the world like a human Elmo from *Sesame Street*. She extended her hand. The girl ignored it, and then spied me, a deer caught in the headlights look in her blue eyes. Poor little fawn. She looked no more than thirteen, with a pregnancy the size of a basketball. I gave her a smile and she flipped me off.

I get that a lot. In the two years I've lived here, I've seen lots of angry, beaten down girls. Sure, for some women St. Mary's is a sad place. They're here because they're pregnant and abandoned, homeless with kids, or beat up by someone they thought they could trust. Usually, when the girls leave, they have hope. Aunt Angela and Mickey work hard to help them see a future.

Aunt Angela tries to work that positive stuff on me, too. She wants me to attend self-esteem workshops and classes she provides about how to interview for a job, things like that. But it ends up being about as much fun for both of us as scraping our knuckles on a cheese grater. The one class I did agree to, self-defense, suited me fine. Knowing how to whip anyone into submission by just getting hold of their little finger is information worth knowing. All that other falderal is crap.

The phone rang again. A boy of about four with a green dyed Mohawk haircut walked by, picked up the phone, then placed it back into its cradle. I smiled and mouthed "good boy" behind Aunt Angela's back. Aunt Angela has an office phone that is never ignored, since it might be someone in trouble on the other end of it. This was the house phone for the girl's personal calls and not so closely monitored.

"Why don't you give Blair a call and get to the bottom of this wedding thing so that phone will stop ringing," Mickey said as she came through the kitchen to get a couple cold drinks for her and the new girl. Aunt Angela and Mickey had been partners for years and co-managed St. Mary's for the diocese. Neither one of them had any hesitancy about trying to manage my life, either.

"Both River and I know my brother wouldn't want either of us at his wedding," said Aunt Angela. "He wrote me off the day I came out and Angus threw me out of the house. No, Blair's got something else up her sleeve, but we're not going to get any peace until you hear her out, River."

"Why don't I just shove my hand in a wood chipper?" I said.

"After you call Blair," said Aunt Angela.

Shit. I stalled as long as I could, folding the brown grocery bags into neat stacks and sliding them into the wire magazine rack we kept for that purpose. When I could no longer tolerate the daggers of ice coming from Aunt Angela's eyes slicing into my back, I reached for the phone.

"Oh, good," Blair whispered when she answered. "You've finally taken a break from that wretched house of ill repute you work in."

"Why are you whispering?" I rubbed my neck with my free hand. "For the love of Mike, this isn't a house of ill repute. It's a women's shelter."

She cleared her throat and kicked up the volume a notch. "I don't want Daddy to hear me. I'll get another lecture on how I'm exceeding my minutes and causing the national debt. I guess

I'm just confused about the whorehouse thing. John told me you were working in some house with a bunch of ruined women. I just assumed…"

"Very funny," I said. Blair would tease me with a water hose if I were on fire. Besides, I knew John wouldn't say that. And, where had she seen my father, anyway? He stays mostly on the Rez. I couldn't imagine she'd go there to seek him out. Pine Ridge Reservation can be a great place to visit from a tour bus, but might be dangerous if you don't know where you're going.

I sighed, pushing the receiver deeper into my shoulder so I could have my hands free. Aunt Angela picked up a breakfast dish one of the kids left on the counter, but cleanup was my job, so I pushed her away and took the plate, scraping jelly off it and managing to get it on the ends of my waist-length hair. Great. I looked around the window ledge and found a rubber band where Aunt Angela usually throws them from the newspaper and quickly fashioned a fat braid. "Okay, Blair, you've got a nanosecond to tell me the real reason you want me to come out there."

"Fair enough. I know you don't like me, but I want that to change. I really, really, do want you and Aunt Angela to come to Daddy's wedding. He's getting married to Ruby Graham. She's some old friend of Aunt Angela's and she'd love to have you at the wedding. She's a little nutty and over-the-top religious. She's nice, and the best thing that's ever happened to Daddy."

"Is that it? You're sticking to that story? 'Cause if that's all you've got, you know I'm saying no."

"C'mon, River. Daddy's not the same man you knew as a child. He's reborn, or saved, or some such thing. It's weird, but Ruby has changed him somehow. She's even got him teaching Sunday school. He's already put an invitation and airplane tickets in the mail for you and Aunt Angela. Says he means to make amends."

How would Colin make amends for the night Blair's mother, my Aunt Bonnie, died? Sure, maybe he was crazed with grief. But, he drove his truck clean through the wall of our living room that night. Mom, John and I barely escaped with our lives when Colin stumbled, bleeding, out of his truck. He cursed and shouted at John to never come near him again, waving a shotgun. I'd never been so scared.

I guess my silence prompted Blair to continue talking. "But, you're right," she said. "That's not the only reason I need you here. Since I graduated, Daddy's been insisting that I learn the administration end of this new Bonnie B Guest Ranch business he's starting instead of going to fashion design school like I want. But Ruby's almost convinced him that I'm all wrong for it. I mean, can you imagine me doing mundane things like keeping supplies stocked and doing payroll?"

Frankly, I couldn't imagine Blair doing an honest day's labor of any kind. "No, I can't," I said.

"I have better things to do with my time, I can tell you."

Like painting your toenails. "I don't see that this has anything to do with me," I said. "So, I'm hanging up now."

I could hear Blair take a deep calming breath. "C'mon, River. Don't." Her voice took on a wheedling quality. "We should support each other. It hasn't been easy for either of us. You know, both of us losing…"

I put my hand to my throat in a strangling gesture. She was going to pull the orphan card.

"…our mothers," she finished.

Aunt Bonnie was my mother's twin. She'd gotten pregnant with Blair the same month my mother got pregnant with me. She died when we were eight, giving birth to Blair's little brother, who also died.

As I silently brooded about my mom and Aunt Bonnie, Blair rushed in to fill the void. "I hate to think of you being stuck away in Kansas at that shelter. You can't be making much money. Come with me to New York while I attend school. Live with me and get a real job."

I couldn't have been more surprised. New York? "Leaving here is out of the question. Besides, Colin will never let you leave Pell Mell to go to New York," I said, attempting to take the focus off me. "He's a control freak. You used to say he didn't ever want you to leave Pell Mell, even to go out of town to college. Isn't it going to tick him off if you go clear across the country?"

"Normally, yes. I'd hate to think he would find some way to get rid of the money Mom left me in trust, but if I give him a hard time, he might. Like give it to charity in my name or something. I don't want to chance it. No, getting him mad is definitely not an option. And, that's where you come in. He will let me go *if* you're my roommate."

"You can't be serious," I said.

"I know. Weird to me, too. I figure it's part of this whole Christian thing he's into now. It's like he's your biggest fan. He's all, 'River's a survivor. River knows how to cook and keep house and she can balance a checkbook.' I could puke when he starts ranting like that. He wants me to learn to run this ranch, but when it comes to living on my own, I guess he thinks I'll forget to pay the phone bill or something. Maybe he thinks if he's not around to monitor my every thought, I'll party all the time."

"Sounds about right," I said. I didn't know what Blair was up to, but I knew Colin didn't want me anywhere near him or his precious daughter. He made that clear years ago. "What am I supposed to do in New York City?" I asked.

"I don't know. If you don't want to get a job, I bet Daddy will pay for your college. If you don't want that, marry a rich stockbroker. C'mon, you're my only hope."

Pay for college? That was rich. Colin wouldn't even take me in when Mom died. "Don't whine," I said. "I'll think about the New York thing." I lied to her just to end this conversation. I had to be straight on one point, though. "No way am I coming to the wedding. There are too many bad memories in Pell Mell for me to ever go back. What would I do if I ran into Billy?"

"Jeez, you are so hardheaded! Talking sense to you is as hard as cracking walnuts with my butt cheeks. Billy did not murder your mother. I've known him all my life. He comes from a very respected family. His daddy is the sheriff of Pell Mell for Pete's sake, and his mother is pastor of Trinity church for crying out loud."

I hung up.

Chapter Two

The conversation with Blair kept ricocheting around my brain. How could she continue to love Billy? How could she be so blasé about what he did to me?

True, we were only kids, eleven and thirteen, when he came at me in the school basement. I was fetching supplies for Mom. She taught fourth grade and I think the kids had eaten all the paste or something. Anyway, I was down there when Billy came at me. I was expecting a practical joke or a new wrestling move. He was always testing them out on me. But, this time he had his wangie hanging out when he pushed me back against the color copier. I whomped him so hard with a printer cartridge even I saw the stars.

Maybe, like he said at the time, he only meant to scare me. Boys are goobers. Truth was, he looked as scared as I felt. He'd gotten into terrible trouble after I ran up the stairs screaming to my mother. His dad, Buster, was having a parent-teacher conference with Mom at the time and he whipped him on the spot. For this little stunt with me, Billy later got six months in juvie. For killing my mother next day, he got zip. Those two events splash together in my memory like poison.

Determined not to give thoughts of Billy any more of my time, I consciously replaced thoughts of him with an old Billy Joel song about how it's my life and people ought to leave me alone. I flung a dirty oatmeal pan harder than I intended into sudsy water and commenced scrubbing. I was distracted by what I saw out the window.

"What's her story?" I asked Mickey, indicating the window as she breezed through the kitchen.

Mickey came over to join me at the window. A cool breeze gently moved the curtain as she peered over my shoulder. "Oh, her? She came in with her little brother and her mom last night, fleeing some gorilla that her mother had the bad taste to shack up with. They took off with nothing but the clothes on their backs and the dirty clothes in their laundry hamper. I showed her where the laundry facilities were."

We both watched as The Girl bent over at the waist with her ass to us, her French cut shorts riding up on her cheeks. "How old is she?" I asked.

"Sixteen."

"Looks a lot older."

"A hard life will do that to you," Mickey said, and left.

I spritzed some cleaner on a rag and wiped down the counters. I was working hard on a bit of yolk that had stuck fast like a big yellow booger when The Girl walked in.

"Hi," she said, placing her muddy plastic laundry basket on my clean counter. I picked up the basket, wiped the counter again, and carried the basket to the laundry folding table in the utility room off the kitchen. "You guys got any soda?" she asked. I fetched a Pepsi for her from the fridge.

"You Indian?" she asked. "I like your cheekbones."

"Half. Mother's white. Thanks," I said.

"So," she said, lowering herself into a chair and sliding her butt forward on the plastic seat, her long legs extended in front of her like the forks on an Orange County chopper. She took a swig of Pepsi. "What's your job around here?"

"I keep busy doing odd jobs," I said. "I do housework and yard work for the shelter. I like it," I added, smiling at her. Trying to make her feel welcome. "Nobody bothers me," I said, letting her know what was important to me.

"Yeah, I'm sure that's true. Wouldn't you like to be bothered a little? Like, booooring."

She handed me her empty can like she was a princess and I should wait on her. I took it and pitched it in the recycle bin.

"So, what's it like?" she asked. "Working for them, I mean? Do they French in front of you?"

I decided to cut her some slack and assume her question came mostly from ignorance and not meanness. If she had attended a backwater school like Pell Mell High, I could understand why she wasn't simpatico with the lesbian lifestyle. Pell Mell High wasn't exactly a cosmopolitan hot spot, with only five hundred kids, split into categories—the Cowboys, the Jocks, the Goths and the Preps. I had my own category when I attended there. I was the "Bitchy Half-Breed."

You'd think prejudice like that wouldn't exist in the twenty-first century, but you'd be wrong. South Dakota history seeps into the present, coloring some people's attitudes, both Indian and white. It's not as bad as it used to be, like in the Seventies when Indians and the FBI were shooting at each other at Wounded Knee. But, there are guys who won't date me because I'm half Indian. These same guys are totally on board if I want to give them ten minutes on my knees behind Grainger's Feed and Seed, though. Anyway, if there are gays at Pell Mell High they never came out, self-preservation being the strongest instinct and all.

"Aunt Angela and Mickey are very businesslike around each other," I said.

"You like girls, too?" she asked.

I turned the water on in the sink and washed my hands and dried them, being sure I placed the towel on the towel bar with the edges together. "Why don't I take a break," I said. "I'll make us a sandwich and we can watch Oprah."

She was game so I slid bologna and cheese with mayonnaise

and white bread onto paper towels and we carried our sandwiches into the great room. We plunked our butts down on the orange and brown flowered couch. Everything in the room was a garage sale buy, from the couch to the chrome dinette with the red Formica top to the old piano. The Assistance League had donated the TV.

Oprah was telling the overworked housewives of America to take time to smell the roses and indulge themselves occasionally. "You like her?" the girl asked.

"She's okay," I said.

"No, I mean do you really like her? Would you like to get next to her? Do her?"

I had about had it with her and her act. I was almost to the point of slapping her sideways when she stopped me with a look, focusing on my lips. "You have just a bit of mayo, right there," she said, putting her sandwich down and sliding to my end of the couch. She put her fingertip on my mouth and pushed in slightly. Then she took her mayo-covered finger and slid it into her mouth. And, my heart nearly stopped.

Next thing I know, she's on top of me and her hips are grinding into mine. Her lips tasted of fruity lip balm and spearmint. She pulled away from me briefly, took gum from her mouth and globbed it onto the end table. The movement caused her peasant blouse to snag on my belt buckle. Her blouse eased down her cleavage and sent up a vanilla scent. Her hand slid under my shirt and cupped my boob. I leisurely wrapped my arm around her shoulders like I did this kind of thing every day and kissed her back.

For awhile I could hear nothing but a loud buzz in my ears. Until Aunt Angela's voice cut through the buzz. "River. My office. Right now!"

The Girl jumped up like a scalded rabbit and ran outside. When I could get my legs to move, I lumbered behind Aunt Angela and took a seat in her office, facing her desk. She closed the door.

"What the Sam Hill was that?" she asked as she paced behind her desk.

"I...I..." Words were forming in my brain, but they weren't

lining up right to fire out my mouth.

"Cheese and Crust." Aunt Angela drew her hand through her hair. "I'm responsible for you, River, and what goes on around here. Why, if Father Boone had been privy to that display, he'd have had an aneurysm on the spot. Are you trying to get me fired?"

I felt myself blush what I knew must be deep crimson.

"I know you've had a hard life. Didn't get much in the way of a moral upbringing." She was beginning a litany I'd heard her recite before.

"Heaven knows I'm partly responsible for that," she said. "I'll never forgive myself for not checking on you sooner after your mother died. I naturally assumed that you'd go to Colin's to live. Mickey and I were so remote, in the Peace Corp in Colombia. I didn't even know Briana had died until after the funeral. With the cholera outbreak and all, we just couldn't get stateside."

Yada Yada. I took a deep breath.

She stopped to cup my chin gently like I was a fragile piece of glass and she thought I might break. "I can still remember how vulnerable you seemed when I took you away from that pathetic foster family. They had you cleaning their toilet with a toothbrush like some G D Cinderella."

If it hadn't been my hide on the line, I would've wished she didn't feel so guilty about me. She's Catholic and suffers from congenital guilt anyway. I didn't think it could hurt to work it. I looked at her with the biggest cow eyes I could muster.

"And, I've come to the conclusion that those foster brothers must have abused you," she continued. "I think that's why you're borderline obsessive compulsive about the cleaning around here."

She looked at me like she expected to me to say something. Maybe get it off my chest. Yeah, they abused me all right, just by being on the same planet as me and me having to breathe the same air. It never was much more than bra popping and wedgies, with the occasional swirly. I always gave as good as I got. They learned it wasn't wise to piss off people who prepare your food.

She sat down, lit up a cigarette and took a long draw. "I just can't tolerate you messing up with that girl. She's only a child, and been through so much. You're of age."

The phone rang and Aunt Angela laid her cigarette on the ashtray. "St. Mary's Shelter," she answered. She put her hand over the receiver and whispered to me, "I have to take this call. Go sit in the great room on the couch. Stay away from her. I'll deal with you in a minute."

I schlepped out of her office and sat down opposite the door, on the couch, thinking about The Girl. I didn't even know her name and I guessed it would probably be good if I never did. Even though my shit was hitting the fan, I could feel a goofy grin trying to break through. I felt like a big piece of the puzzle of my life had snapped into place.

I could hear Aunt Angela's voice, a murmur now and then, rising and falling, but none of the words. When I saw her pace past the door, my breath caught. All the color had drained from her face and I saw her steady herself against the desk. She saw me looking at her and nudged the door shut with her foot.

After about five minutes, she called me in. "Everything okay?" I asked. "You look pale. Was that rotten Blair again? What'd she say?"

"Oh, that? That was nothing. Just Father Boone with some budget issues. Speaking of Blair brings to mind her invitation. I got a call from Ruby early this morning." Aunt Angela sat down and posed her hands in a steeple. "I think it'd be good for me to take a break from all this and visit my old friend. I sure as H E double hockey sticks am not going to leave you here with That Girl. So, I've decided you and I are going to South Dakota for Ruby's wedding."

Could things get worse?

"By the way, Ruby mentioned your sister has gone and gotten herself pregnant. She wants you to talk to her while we're there and try to get her to come back here and put the baby up for adoption."

Yes, they could.

That was the day a lot of things came together for me. And this was the moment things began to fall apart.

Chapter Three

Some interesting mental images of a girl getting herself pregnant popped into my head. I pondered the urban myth about a virgin getting pregnant in a swimming pool. How do these things get started? I shook my head. I'd be more likely to believe that, though, than my special needs sister getting pregnant. Yes, she's pretty. And sure, guys like her. But, the Mandy I know is too childlike to be interested in them. Had she been raped?

Mandy is John's child, my half sister, by another mother. She was born with fetal alcohol syndrome which causes her to look at the world through eighteen-year-old eyes and interpret the information received through a brain that stopped evolving at about age eight.

Her birth meant big-time trauma for my mom. Mom was married to John at the time, and pregnant with me. She threw him out. But then, one day he showed up with Mandy.

He said it was over with Mandy's mother. That she had

taken off with no forwarding address. He told Mom he couldn't bear to give the baby up and he needed her help. He told her he loved her. Mom took him back, at least for awhile. She never held it against Mandy when John and she finally broke for good, maintaining custody of Mandy even after the divorce because of John's drinking.

Then, Mom got murdered and we got dumped. The upside to that creepy foster family that we got placed with was that they coddled Mandy like she was some kind of pet. When Aunt Angela finally sought custody, I didn't want to leave Mandy behind. Aunt Angela wanted me and I was desperate to leave. She would have taken Mandy, too, but Mandy wanted to stay with the foster family.

I fingered my necklace, a birthday gift from my sister when I was ten. The silver heart felt smooth under my fingertips, but I could still make out the word *Friends* engraved on it. It had a jagged edge like it had been torn apart. Mandy had kept the other part that said *Forever.* I wanted to help her, but going back...where Mom died...

Mickey sashayed in and plopped herself into the desk chair beside me, bringing me back to the present.

"What if I refuse to go back?" I asked, a chip teetering on my shoulder.

"We'll fire your ass," she said. "Thanks for calling me with a heads up on this, hon," she said to Aunt Angela.

"Now, now, no call for talk like that—yet." Aunt Angela walked over to the old Mr. Coffee on the file cabinet and poured two cups of coffee. One she creamed and handed to Mickey. "River, I'm gonna give it to you like this. You either go with me, or I'm making you a Lamaze coach for one of the girls, to be there for her clear through the messy delivery. I'll schedule some counseling sessions for you with Father Boone. You can stay at the rectory visiting quarters with the nuns while I'm gone and commute from Clear Creek. Father Boone's a heck of a guy. Easy to talk to. I know how the Church is about gays, but even I can talk to Father Boone. He doesn't think me and Mickey being gay affects our ability to run this shelter."

"If you think you'll just run away because you're eighteen,

think again," said Mickey. "We can press charges for some trumped up thing with that little tart. We'll have the law after you."

I shivered, wondering if they could really do that since I was eighteen and The Girl was sixteen, or if Mickey was bluffing.

I considered my options. Believe me, childbirth was not something I relished watching firsthand. I gave them both a dark look. Be damned before I'd talk to Father Boone, the old coot. And staying with the nuns? "Oh, all right!" I said and stomped out. I heard them both giving each other a high five behind my back as I walked out and wondered why Aunt Angela was so hot on going to South Dakota when she had been so opposed to it before.

I picked up the kitchen phone and called Blair. Screw Aunt Angela if she complained the phone bill was too high. "You don't need to call again," I said. "We're coming to the stupid wedding."

I could hear her giggling and clapping. "Good, good," she said. "When you get here, be on your best behavior. I want Daddy to think you're the responsible citizen he has you pegged for so I can get out of this dump."

"I never said I was going to New York."

"That's okay. You will. I'll talk you into it."

"One thing," I said. "You better tell your friend Billy to steer clear of me."

"I wondered how long it would take before Billy came up," she said. "Geesh, give the guy a break. He never did—"

"Stop it! Stop right now," I said. Swear to God if I could've reached through the phone and strangled her, I would have. I slid down the wall I was leaning against and rested on my haunches. "I realize that you'd defend Billy if he were standing over my dead body with an ax. He's bad, Blair." I thought of the last time I'd seen Billy when he was thirteen, being hauled off to juvie. After I read about the detention center in the book *Holes*, I fervently hoped that they had put him someplace like that.

I accidentally knocked over a pile of mail Aunt Angela had dropped on a chair by the phone, and I fingered through it. I ripped open an envelope with Bonnie B Ranch as the return address. "I see the tickets came today," I said. I popped them out. I could feel those little pissed off frown lines forming around my mouth again. "Looks like we leave day after tomorrow."

"I can't wait," said Blair. "Daddy and Ruby are so looking forward to seeing you both."

I made a very unladylike snort into the phone. "You know that old phrase, when pigs fly? Well, I think the whole barnyard would have to be in the air before I would believe Colin would want me anywhere near him or his family."

I could hear exasperation in Blair's voice. "You're such a twerp. Why would you say that?"

"Because he dislikes me. And John. Because we're Native," I said, stating what I felt was obvious. "Don't you remember his childhood nickname for me? Little Squaw Squat-To-Pee?"

"It's not Indians my dad dislikes," she said. "It's just John. Your father is creepy. All that mumbo jumbo shaman stuff he's into. Grandpa always said—"

"Don't talk to me about what Angus says."

"Grandfather Angus, don't you mean? Let me hear you say it—Grandfather Angus Mckee," she said.

"Fat chance," I said. "I can hardly call someone grandfather who won't even acknowledge I exist."

She was silent for a moment. "Point taken. He was always a shit to you. Anyway, he's got nothing to say about what I do. He's just a sick old man. Daddy runs everything now."

"By now, Colin's probably a carbon copy of that old man," I said. "Does your dad shoot stray cats for sport like Angus did?"

"Listen, River. Daddy's not the same man you knew as a child," Blair insisted.

"Oh, save it for someone who cares. See you in a couple days."

Chapter Four

That airplane is too small, I thought as I eyed the toy-looking craft that was supposed to fly us to Rapid City. I looked around at my doomed co-passengers. "We can't all fit in that," I said. I heard a thin whine thread itself through my voice. "There's no way this thing can fly," I insisted. "It looks like an egg carton with wings."

We had left the shelter to go to the airport as the sun was coming up. It was early June, which usually brings breezes to the plains. Not today. My skin was sticky, like I'd ladled styling gel on it. I had on jeans and a standard white Catholic school blouse I'd fished out from a box of clothes the nuns had brought over. I hadn't had time for breakfast, and the jet fuel fumes wafting across the runway made my stomach queasy.

"Gee, no one could tell this is your first time in an airplane. Just relax," Aunt Angela said.

We walked outside the terminal to board the airplane. I put my foot on the first step of the rollaway steel staircase that led to the airplane door. Its gaping mouth yawned at the top of the steps, revealing a shadowed interior. How could I relax? It wasn't just the airplane. I had always thought if there was anyone I could count on to be consistent, it was Aunt Angela. "You know, usually when you say no, you mean no," I said. "Not this time. You say no, then you change your mind about this trip and insist you and I go. Aren't you concerned that Angus might be at this wedding?"

"He's a man full of hate all right," said Aunt Angela, coming up the stairs behind me. "I hope I don't see him. Colin is the only kid he didn't disown. If I have to face him, I will. This trip may give us both closure, River. I never really felt you came to terms with, you know, Briana's accident."

I looked back over my shoulder and gave her an aggrieved look. "Accident! I saw Billy point a gun at Mom and force her off the cliff." The person behind Aunt Angela looked so startled that I remained silent until we were seated.

"Honey, you were only eleven," said Aunt Angela as we tucked ourselves in the tiny seats. "Do you think it's possible you were so traumatized, your brain doesn't remember events as they actually took place? That park was an accident waiting to happen. Even though that area was roped off, they should never have taken a class full of children up there."

That point was certainly valid. Pell Mell was not known for its kinder, gentler school system. Our playground had concrete under the swings and monkey bars and slides, not the sand or chipped wood schools have today. Our food at the cafeteria was cooked up in lard. If we'd been an African village, the teachers would have tied ropes around our waists and used us for gator bait.

"Not true. Billy killed her," I said.

She smoothed her finger over a twitchy eyelid. "Stop putting up such a fuss."

I wasn't buying that this trip wasn't upsetting her. I'd seen her hand tremble when she hung up the phone that day she was supposedly talking to Father Boone. Something was up. "You can pretend everything is hunky-dory if you want. But, don't believe I buy this for a minute," I said. I scowled at her and made a tsk-tsk sound. "Shame on you for lying." She didn't flinch. No way to shame her into being truthful.

As the little aircraft pulled itself into the heavens, I could almost hear, I think I can, I think I can, coming from the engine. I spent my time gripping the armrest and saying Hail Mary's. Aunt Angela spent her time fidgeting and generally driving me nuts. She accidentally dropped her nicotine gum in the toilet and was in full-blown withdrawal about an hour into the flight, alternately complaining that she was going to die if she didn't get a cigarette, or her skin was going to fly off her body at any moment. Since we'd been delayed in our takeoff because of some engine problem, it had been four hours since her last cigarette. Finally, thank God, the wheels touched down at Rapid City Airport before I resorted to throwing her or myself off the plane.

As I deplaned, the wind caught my braid, smacking me in the face, but the air was fresh and clean and a break from the humidity of Clear Creek. I stepped from the metal staircase onto the airstrip and engine noise from other jets assaulted my eardrums. I had expected to be delivered via a walkway to a terminal building, but it appeared we were all in for a walk outside. A man in an orange vest wearing big blue ear defenders led our little group of travelers across the concrete. As we walked toward the terminal building, I could see Blair waving a slender arm at us from a huge window above me. Midday sunlight flowed around her like an angelic aura. Talk about a study in contrasts.

Ear defender man led us to a door in the terminal building that opened onto a staircase. We trudged our carry-on bags up the steps like good little passengers. Inside the building, the soles of my worn tennis shoes sank into the gray carpet as blessedly the door slammed shut behind me and the noise stopped. We walked through the secured area to the main area where everyone was allowed to congregate. Fluorescent light glinted off shiny silver and black chairs, hooked together like train cars. Travelers milled about, eating on the run, looking in shops or waiting for luggage. Blair stood in front of a coffee shop. She smiled and tossed a coffee cup into the trash and walked toward us.

"I gotta say," Blair said as she approached, "you do have a way with that high cheekbone, Southwestern thing you do. I love the braid." She gave me a hug then looked me up and down. "But, we've got to do something about your wardrobe." She was so slender and tiny, I felt like a moose dancing with a gazelle.

"You look good," I said, and meant it.

"Who's the hired help you brought with you?" Blair asked as she shrugged toward Aunt Angela.

Aunt Angela smiled and replied, "Don't give me your stuff, Blair. Give your old auntie a hug, then a cigarette. I'm about to lose my flippin' mind."

Blair reached into her leather bag and pulled out a pack of Virginia Slims. She offered one to Aunt Angela. "Here ya go," she said. "Don't smoke that here," she cautioned. "There's a restaurant with a smoking area if you don't want to wait until we get to the parking lot. It'll be a minute before they get the bags off the plane, anyway."

The clicking of coffee cups and amiable conversation floated over to us, mingled with the comforting smell that can only come from a good greasy cheeseburger and onion rings. "I could use a little something to eat. How about you, Aunt Angela?" I said.

"Forget that," Blair said. "We've got time for a quick smoke, but we really don't have time for a meal." She turned on her heel and started down the corridor. Aunt Angela and I picked up our carry-on luggage and trudged behind her. When we came to a place called Crazy Horse Lounge, we found chairs at a cocktail bar and sat down near a guy wearing a Mt. Rushmore visor cap. I looked longingly at his plate of chicken fried steak as Aunt Angela and Blair took some quick puffs. When he looked up at me and smiled, my stomach did a dive. For a split second I thought it was Billy. But of course I was mistaken. Stupid, stupid, stupid. Was I going to see him in everyone and everywhere?

Blair and Aunt Angela snuffed out their cigarettes after a couple minutes of friendly banter, and I grabbed a few coasters with pictures of South Dakota Jackalopes on them for souvenirs. As we walked out of the restaurant toward the luggage turntable, I assured myself that the chances of seeing Billy were slim. He was probably already back in jail for being caught facedown in some lady's panty drawer. My neck muscles relaxed a little as I wrestled our suitcases off the turntable and looked at Blair to point me in the right direction.

"You're gonna love this ride," she said as we walked passed several parked cars in the lot. We approached a lemon yellow Mustang convertible with a sticker on its shiny chrome bumper: I'll Knock The Crap Out Of Your Honor Student. "This is it," Blair said. I heard a tiny beep as she pressed a button on her keychain, heard a pop, and saw the trunk door rise.

"Hot car," I said as I wedged our bags into the trunk. Blair smiled her Paris Hilton, I-have-it-all smile at me, and flipped her hair over her shoulder. I opened the car door and folded my legs under me on the butter cream leather upholstery, sitting in the backseat so Aunt Angela could be in front and have more room. Blair pulled levers and pushed a button and the top came down. We exited the lot and Blair pushed the car up to ninety.

Bonnie B Ranch, named for Blair's mother, stretched over a few hundred acres about sixty miles east of the Rapid City airport. To the west were the Black Hills, sacred to the Lakota, covered with pine trees so dense and dark the hills looked black from a distance. The terrain on the east side of the state was flat, opened to grazing land and interstate highways. In no time Blair had the car flying over the flatland, evidently trying for her personal best at the land speed record.

"Are we in a hurry?" I yelled at her over the sound of the wind.

"Yes," she yelled back over her shoulder. "Ruby and Daddy are having a big party tonight. All of Ruby's crazy relatives are coming. After all, it's a big deal when the last remaining virgin in a family marries at age forty-three. She's been bugging me to help set up."

"Why don't you drop us at a motel in Pell Mell," Aunt Angela said. "We don't want to intrude while they're entertaining."

"Don't be ridiculous. Daddy can't wait to see you both," said Blair.

Aunt Angela and I looked at each other and shrugged. "Fat chance," she mouthed. The wind caught her words and blew them down the road.

I took a deep breath and hugged myself, suppressing a shiver. I wasn't cold. I couldn't put my finger on what this feeling was. It was different than the anxiety I felt at the prospect of seeing Colin again. Something seemed off. No one else appeared to notice anything amiss. I was probably just hungry. Low blood sugar making me freaky.

Blair's hair flowed behind her like a banshee in flight, and she and Aunt Angela went deep into conversation about something. Hair, makeup, clothes? I wasn't paying attention until she mentioned Hannibal Lake.

"Daddy's building some guest cabins out there," she was saying, "and putting in camping spots and RV hookups. He's having swimming beaches developed. You know the cliff where, well, you know."

Aunt Angela gave her a hard stare and looked at me. "Yeah, I know," she said.

Blair continued, "He's having a bridge put across that ravine and some hiking trails marked underneath it."

So. Strangers would be tramping over the place my mother had lain twisted and bleeding, under the cliff's edge. Would Colin put up a marker, at least, in her honor? I shook myself. If I was going to survive this trip I was going to have to make my thoughts behave.

"Is Colin giving up the cattle operation?" Aunt Angela asked.

"No. He'll have that and the horses, too. Most of them are this side of the glue factory but we'll use them for trail rides for the tourists. I still have Darkwater, of course."

Blair had gotten her beautiful black horse shortly before I left Pell Mell. The first time I saw him I was sure he looked directly into my soul with those dark eyes. I saw his, too. I knew he was too much horse for Blair. I'd been right. According to John, that horse had kicked more ass than Jackie Chan.

I was convinced the fault lay with Blair and Colin and not the horse. I knew I could ride Darkwater. It had been too long since I had ridden a good horse and I was sure I could handle him. "Can I ride him?" I shouted up to Blair. I was like a five-year-old asking for a lollipop.

She pushed her designer sunglasses up on her nose. "Sure, if you crave some whoop ass. No one's had much luck taming him. Daddy's been using him for stud. I talked him into hiring this very good horse whisperer I know. It won't be long until he's as easy as a merry-go-round pony." That worried me. I hated to think someone would break that beautiful horse's spirit.

As the car sailed forward, the morning sun reflected off the blacktop ahead of us like pools of quicksilver. The glare made it difficult to focus, but my eyes zoomed in on a lone figure walking up ahead. "Blair, is that Mandy? Stop. Stop!"

"Not a chance. That skank can walk," Blair said as she flipped her cigarette to the road.

I reached forward from the backseat and not so softly squeezed her shoulder, digging in my nails a little. "Stop for her," I insisted.

"Cut it out!" she said, but she slowed the car and pulled over. Mandy turned toward us. Her worn maternity top was clean, but stained yellow under the armpits, no doubt by several other pregnant women who'd worn it before her. She wore white maternity shorts. Little strappy sandals barely contained her swollen feet.

"Hey, Mandy, want to ride?" I called as I stepped out of the car and walked toward her. I was sure she couldn't get much more mileage out of those shoes.

Mandy put her hand up to shade her eyes. "Who is that?" she said. Her face broke into a grin. "Is that my River? River!" she shouted as she waddled to me, arms open wide. I caught her in a hug and, standing eye to eye, she kissed my face in several places. "Oh, River, I dreamed you was dead. I'm so glad you're not. Step back and let me look." She held me at arm's length. "You're gorgeous." She picked up my braid and tickled her chin with the end of it. "I thought you was dead."

"Of course I'm not dead." I ran my hand through her short thick brown hair. Why would you think such a thing?"

"I heard Billy tell Blair you were dead meat," she said. I glared at Blair. Her eyes drifted to a piece of lint on her dress that she flipped off with her hand. "Billy's wrong," I said.

Mandy's amber eyes glistened and her smile showed

straight, white teeth. Her too wide nose, much like John's, was covered with a dark pigmented patch that extended across her high cheekbones, giving her a sweet, panda look. I had seen that happen to other pregnant girls at the shelter. "You look wonderful," she said.

"You're gorgeous, too," I said, as we walked toward the car. "Being pregnant agrees with you. Why didn't you let me know you were going to have a baby? You never called me after I left. You never took my calls."

She stopped walking and looked straight into my eyes and moved to about an inch from my face. Violating personal space had never been a consideration for Mandy. "I don't like to use telephones. Remember when Effie Crow was talking on one and got hit by lightning? She died. I don't want that to happen to me and my baby."

"That seldom happens," I said. "Only when there is a thunderstorm going on."

"Yes, but there's always a thunderstorm going on somewhere," she said, her eyes wide.

I gave up. "You and I need to visit before I go back to Clear Creek. Okay?"

"Silly, gorgeous girl," she said. "I'll see you every day. I'll be at the Bonnie B because I work there." She squeezed her eyes shut. My mom had tried to teach her to wink with one eye, but this two-eyed squeeze was as close as she could come. "I'm on my way to the ranch to help Ruby," she continued. "Lots to do." She turned to Blair. "My Auntie Liz only drives me as far as the crossroads, then I have to walk. It's only a half mile, but I'm so tired of walking. Thanks for stopping for me, Blair."

"Shut up, ho, and get in," said Blair.

"You stop that, Blair!" Mandy commanded and landed a resounding slap on Blair's cheek. "That's bad language."

"Why you bitch! I hate you," Blair screamed as she jumped out of the car and swung at Mandy.

"Stop it this instant!" I yelled at Blair.

Amazingly agile for a person about to give birth to, I swear, triplets, Mandy managed to sidestep Blair's slap.

"Cut it out, you two," Aunt Angela said as I pried Blair and

Mandy apart. That effort got me a kick in the knee. All my instincts screamed at me right then to make Blair turn the car around and take me back to the airport. Like a fool, I didn't listen.

Chapter Five

"Mandy, you get in the back with River," commanded Aunt Angela. "Blair, get in and drive. I'm not about to let you leave Mandy trudging up this road in her condition."

Blair plopped herself in the driver's seat in a huff. She gave me a withering look as she glanced back to check traffic and pulled onto the road. I stuck out my tongue. She spun the tires, spewing gravel behind us like water from a hose.

We traveled in silence until a right turn off the main highway took us to the tree-lined drive that led to the ranch. We passed through a wrought iron gate that reminded me of pictures I'd seen of the entrance to Graceland. *Bonnie B Guest Ranch* was spelled out in ornate curlicues within the frame of the gate. Up ahead, the old ranch house I had known had been replaced by a modern sprawling lodge.

"Wow," I said.

"Told you we'd done renovations," Blair said. "Daddy plans to have the first guests arrive in October. Kind of a run-through for next year's full season. We still have a lot to do." Obvious pride sounded in her voice, and I wondered if she was as committed as she seemed to the move to New York. Rustic split rail fencing on each side of the road flashed by. Black Angus cattle wandered in pastures on either side. We pulled to the front of the ranch house along a gravel drive and Blair stopped the car and popped the trunk. "Mandy, get out. Take the luggage around to the back door," she commanded.

"Not in her condition," Aunt Angela said, her voice thinly covering impatience. "River and I will get them." Mandy patted Aunt Angela's hand in a grateful gesture as she got out of the car.

"Whatev," said Blair, as Aunt Angela and I unloaded luggage from the trunk. "I'll get the 'Stang gassed up and take it back to the garage. Ring the bell. Ruby's in there somewhere."

We carried our luggage across the lawn to the front entrance. The door was unlocked and we entered onto a large glassed-in porch. Adirondack chairs were positioned across the wood plank floor to afford the best view of the prairie. A table between two of the chairs held a chess set with cowboy-themed chess pieces. Hides that obviously used to be on some kind of animal were spread on the floor. A fountain made of an old-fashioned water pump flowed into a basin formed of assorted river stones and took up one end of the room. Water gurgled peacefully as we set our luggage by two double doors that protected the entrance from the porch into the rest of the house.

Aunt Angela looked tired as she sat on the edge of the fountain and dipped her fingers in the water and then rubbed them across her forehead. Mandy looked done in as well and with a grunt lowered her bulk onto a chair. I spied a cowbell by the door, and assuming it was some kind of rustic door knocker, gave the rope a jangle. No one responded to its raucous clang. I heard no activity inside and when I knocked no one came to let us in. I clanged the bell again, then hunched my shoulders. "You two sit here and rest a minute. I'll go around back and see if I can find anybody."

The path to the back of the ranch house wound through an herb garden on one side of the sidewalk and a bulb garden on the side near the house. Brightly colored iris in lavenders, browns, yellows and blues provided a riot of color. The day was warming and sage and rosemary from the herb garden smelled earthy and clean. A small wrought iron bench was nestled amongst the herbs and I was tempted to plop my butt down and spend the rest of the day there staring up at the blue sky. I didn't look forward to seeing Colin. I pushed myself forward anyhow.

As I rounded the corner, I saw the back patio area had been set with a few banquet tables under pink and white striped awnings. Other round tables, adorned with white linen tablecloths and placed with four chairs each, were situated between the house and a huge blue swimming pool and pool house. Green plants and large rocks formed a ledge over which a small waterfall cascaded into the swimming pool from an adjoining whirlpool. Beyond that was an orchard of spindly black trees bearing some kind of nut, maybe pecan. "Toto," I said to myself, "I don't think we're at St. Mary's anymore."

Nestled back into the trees, two small goats shared a pen. As I was looking at them, a large collie ran at them, barking. The goats went stiff and fell over like they'd been flash frozen. "Fainting goats," I said and laughed. I had heard of, but had never seen, goats that when startled fell over stiff-legged into a trance. In a few seconds, they had recovered, until the dog barked and rushed them again. I could tell by the dog's satisfied swagger that this was a game he enjoyed immensely. "You better quit that," I said. "Karma may bite you in the butt." I scratched the knobby bump on the top of his head.

Through an open window, I could hear a radio playing an old gospel hymn that I remembered my mother singing, *What a Friend We Have in Jesus*. The sweet aroma of apples cooking with cinnamon floated to me. I walked over to the door and took a few deep breaths, hesitating to knock and be perhaps face to face with Colin.

Then the door swung out, nearly knocking me off my feet. Out stepped a Humvee of a woman. Her bulky frame was covered by a red shirtwaist dress printed with little yellow flowers and cinched at the waist by a white apron. Cap sleeves emphasized freckled arms. Knee-high nylons, rolled down like bobby socks, peeked out of white oxfords. Wispy tendrils of red hair escaped the bun fashioned at the nape of her neck. The collie took off on a run, and I could tell that karma, in the form of this woman, had already had a swipe or two at him.

"Friskie, stay away from those goats!" she said. When she noticed me, she drew a hand white with flour across her forehead and studied me. "Land a' Goshen, it's River!" She threw her beefy arms around my shoulders and gave me a squeeze. "I've seen pictures of you as a child, but honey, you're all grown up. Pretty. Come on in."

She pulled me through the mud room and into the kitchen, talking nonstop. "Let me get these out, hon," she said as she pulled pies from the oven. "Colin told me to have the party catered. But I couldn't do that. I've got family coming. What would they say? They'd say they want some of Ruby's pies and Ruby's cooking, that's what. Oh, excuse me. You must be starved. I know all you get on airlines is peanuts, if that. By the way, I'm Ruby."

This was Ruby? I managed to fit in a "nice to meet you," before she placed a slab of warm apple pie in front of me, and kept talking. This wasn't the type of woman I would have expected Colin to be attracted to. She was homely. Almost scary. But there was something about her. A smile full of light. Kind eyes. If Colin could love a woman like Ruby, maybe he had changed.

Her voice became a pleasant drone as I surveyed this hi-tech kitchen. Two ovens, two ranges and a side-by-side refrigerator in shiny stainless steel stood ready to serve. Sunlight glinted off assorted copper pots that hung from ceiling beams. Fresh lettuce, carrots, tomatoes and radishes were piled up beside various slicers, dicers and choppers on the granite counters. Cuts of meat were thawing on a stainless steel draining board. The sound of Ruby's voice, the gospel music, fatigue and the aroma of pie lulled me into a comfortable haze of contentment. When I tasted the pie, I was darn near orgasmic. Ruby was a pie goddess.

"So, where's your sweet auntie?" She asked. "Couldn't she come?"

"Oh, crap," I said. "I was so hungry, I forgot Aunt Angela and Mandy. They're on the porch by the fountain."

"Land a' Goshen. You mean that Blair didn't even bring you all in? That girl! I swear, sometimes...Well, let's go get 'em," she said.

Ruby bustled through the house to the front door and I followed along. She burst through the double doors and grabbed Aunt Angela's thin torso and gave her a squeeze. I almost lost sight of Aunt Angela's head in Ruby's ample cleavage. Mandy sniffed the air and made a beeline for the kitchen.

"Oh, my darlin' dear. Here you are. I was afraid you wouldn't come," Ruby said. She lowered her voice. "I know things haven't been the best between you and Colin."

Aunt Angela pulled away from Ruby and ran her hands over her shirt as if she were ironing out wrinkles with her hands. "As I get older," Aunt Angela said, "I've come to realize things that were important then aren't so important now. I hope Colin and I can work things out."

"Good," Ruby said, and beamed. "C'mon into the kitchen. Talk with me while I cook."

We followed Ruby to the kitchen and Aunt Angela glanced at me as we settled ourselves onto leather café stools at a bar beside Mandy, who was busy devouring pie. After Ruby set frosty glasses of cold sweet tea before us, Aunt Angela addressed me. "Ruby and I met years ago when Angus tossed me out," she said. "Mickey and I didn't have a dime. We moved into this old building with rats big as cats. Ruby was our neighbor across the hall. Remember that old apartment building, Ruby?"

"Lord knows I've tried to forget it," Ruby said as she slid some pie in front of Aunt Angela. "You two were so poor it's a wonder you didn't starve. Good thing Mickey at least knew how to play that guitar. Unless I forget, she supported you two for a few months doing the odd gig, folk songs being big then and all."

"I probably wouldn't have eaten without her. And you. You made the best enchiladas in the universe, which you graciously shared with us."

"Still do," Ruby said.

"Did you ever get that nursing certificate you were working toward?" asked Aunt Angela.

"Yes. In fact, I'm a live-in nurse right now for your daddy." She pursed her lips and tiny little puckers appeared under her nose. "He's a cranky old thing. Poor old soul won't even leave the house anymore. I guess that would make anyone cranky. I'm glad I took the job, though. That's how I met Colin."

Aunt Angela's expression hardened. "That old coot deserves to be cranky. Didn't give me a thing the day I left." She looked embarrassed for a moment at her own outburst. "Oh, I didn't care about his money, but I couldn't even take my own things or the few things I knew Momma wanted me to have. I guess Colin will get it all when Angus passes on."

Ruby gave Aunt Angela a sideways glace while she chopped up carrots and arranged them on a tray. "Don't worry about that, Angela. God has a way of making everything come right eventually. Anything in particular you're thinking you should have? When Angus passes, I'll see you get it."

"I don't want anything from that man," Aunt Angela said, "except what's already mine. Besides, he's too mean to ever die."

"Well, just say he did. Ain't none of us can cheat the Grim Reaper. What would it be that you consider yours that you'd want back?" asked Ruby.

Aunt Angela scratched the tip of her nose. "Oh, I don't want to parade the dirty family laundry in front of you right now. You have other things to think about."

"No, now, tell me. I'm part of this family now. Or soon will be. Tell me what you want."

"Well, since you asked." Aunt Angela took the last bite of pie and dropped the fork onto her plate. "I consider the Caitlen crucifix mine. It was handed down from a forebearer who bought it for his wife sometime in the seventeenth century. It belonged to my mother, and it was supposed to be passed on to me as the eldest child."

I put my hands to my neck and made a choking sound. "Please, don't get her talking about that necklace," I said.

"Why not?" Ruby asked.

Aunt Angela looked at me and shook her head. "Don't pay any attention to that brat. She's just commenting on the fact that she's heard this story maybe once before."

"I've heard about that necklace more than once I can assure you," I said.

"What necklace?" Blair asked as she entered the room.

"It's one your Grandma Birdie promised to Angela," said Ruby. "Quite valuable, I'm guessing."

"I wish someone had promised me something valuable," said Blair. "I could use the money for New York."

"Oh? Has River agreed to go with you, then?" asked Ruby.

Blair gave me a poke in the belly with her finger. "She will, even if I have to torture her," she said.

"You torture me enough every time you open your mouth," I said, but tempered it with a smile. Blair threw a carrot stick at me.

"Sorry," said Ruby. "I haven't seen anything like that necklace, and I've been through most everything out there since the Buttrams left. Remember them? They were caretakers at the time of Birdie's death? Anyway, Angus told me anything valuable that belonged to Birdie, he had them bundle up and put in safekeeping at the bank. Then, more recently, he gave Mandy instructions to sort through the rest of Birdie's old costume jewelry, take what she wanted, and give the rest to the Goodwill. Mandy was having a hard time making decisions all by herself, so I pitched in. I didn't see anything like a valuable necklace."

"I doubt that Angus knows what happened to it," said Aunt Angela, looking unperturbed. "Momma told me she hid it for me. Momma was good at hiding things. I'm sure it's somewhere in that big old house. She died soon after I left, before she had a chance to get it to me. Who knows what else she hid. Angus kept her a near prisoner in that house. Hiding things was the only way she could keep anything for herself."

"It's just a shame some women let men..." Blah, blah, yadda, yadda. Ruby's and Aunt Angela's conversation drifted into a discussion of the inequities between the sexes and I didn't want to listen. But as they continued to talk, I could see they were truly fond of one another. Was this why Aunt Angela seemed compelled to come after all? To see her old friend marry? Or, talk her out of it?

The rumbling of a diesel engine interrupted the reunion. Out the kitchen window I could see a black truck with tinted windows and the biggest tires I'd ever seen pulling up to park by the goat pen. It was covered in mud. I could barely make out EAT BEEF printed across the vanity plate.

"There's my man now," Ruby cooed. "He'll be tickled to see you two."

I saw Aunt Angela jump at the sound of Colin slamming the truck door. We heard him swearing as he came toward the house. When he entered the mud room through the screen door, he threw it open with such force that it hit the wall.

"Goodness! Whatever is the matter?" Ruby called to him.

"Damned weirdos are after my cattle again, Ruby," he said as he made scuffling noises that sounded like he was pulling off his boots in the mud room. "They gutted two of them out in the south pasture. If I ever find out who those deviants are, I'll stick a cattle prod up...Well, look what the cat dragged in," he said when he finally entered the kitchen and noticed Aunt Angela and me. He took wide strides across the room in his sock feet and hugged an incredulous Aunt Angela. Then, he turned to me. I was totally unprepared for what he did next. "River, you sweet thing," he said, and picked me up, flinging my feet off the ground and spinning me around. No small matter. I'm five foot eight. My feet seldom leave the ground.

Aunt Angela's mouth hung open. I shut my own mouth, realizing I was doing the same thing. Colin, bulkier than I remembered, was dressed in dirty blue jeans and a white wife beater T-shirt, with a belt buckle the size of Ruby's pie plates. His full shock of strawberry-blond hair was now salted with gray. His skin, a dusky red color from too much sun, caused his blue eyes to look even bluer. He had the muscled look of a man used to throwing steers to the ground. Not knowing what to say, I didn't say anything. He set me back on the stool and smiled like he wanted to tickle my chin and say 'kootchie coo.' My awkward silence was interrupted by the sound of Ruby throwing meat onto a sizzling pan.

Aunt Angela finally asked, "What did you mean about the cattle, Colin?"

His jaw tightened. He frowned and balled his fists like he wanted to push them into someone's face. It looked to me like his newfound love for Jesus was going to do a one-eighty. Then he forced his fingers apart and let his hands relax at his side. He took a deep breath. "Some devil-worshiping cult, Buster thinks," he said. I stiffened at the name of Billy's father, Sheriff Buster Chance.

"They're mutilating cows, cats, dogs, anything with a heart," Colin continued. "Lately I've been finding cattle opened up, organs missing. Buster says they probably use them for some kind of satanic sacrifice. Sick sonsabitches." He shook his head, and rubbed his calloused hand across his chin stubble. He looked into Ruby's clearly concerned eyes and something passed between them. "But, let's not talk about that unpleasantness now. I want to hear about how my sis and niece have been getting along."

Aunt Angela and I looked at each other. *Could this be the same man who had not spoken to us in years?* "Hold up a minute," said Aunt Angela. "What is this all about? Hugging us? Inviting us to a wedding when we haven't heard from you in years? What do I make of your behavior?"

Colin looked at his feet for a moment, then he looked heavenward like there was someone on the ceiling he was talking to. "The good Lord saw fit to show me the error of my ways, little sister. I was born again. The old man is passed away. Behold the new man."

Hallefrickinlujah, I thought.

"I do regret the way I have lived my life," Colin continued, "but with the help of this good woman here, in the future I will be a better man." He looked at Ruby like she was a brand-new Harley Davidson, and she beamed back at him. The romantic moment was spoiled for me when he said, "But, damn, if I catch those deviants who are after my cattle, I will kill them."

"We can only hope," said Ruby, shaking her head, as she brought the meat cleaver she was wielding down with a thud, its blade biting into fresh meat. "We can only hope and pray those assholes see the light before God smites 'em."

Chapter Six

Mandy and I played rock, paper, scissors while Ruby, Aunt Angela and Colin gave each other condensed updates of the last few years.

"I really hate to leave you fine ladies," Colin said as he rose from the barstool and slapped Ruby on the butt. "I have to get those carcasses up before the wolves find them. I don't want those scavengers coming in too close to the ranch house." He walked out the door with a wave.

"Mandy, it's time for you to go to work," Ruby said.

"Yes'm. Thanks for the pie." Mandy lowered her eyes as she slid off the stool and washed her plate and fork, then got busy washing vegetables.

To us, Ruby said, "You both look tired and like you could use a nap. Let me show you where you'll be bedding down." Ruby looked around for a hand towel and finding none, wiped her hands on her apron. "If you want a nap before the shindig, I'll make sure no one bothers you. River, you'll take Blair's room.

After the way she left her own relatives standing outside, she's staying in the pool house."

"Oh, I don't want to put anybody out," I said. "I can stay in the pool house." I surely didn't want to make Blair any more ornery than she was already. It would make our two-week stay seem like forever.

"Now, you'll do no such." Ruby shook her head and a bobby pin flew out. "Blair will be fine. If you ask me, that child needs to be inconvenienced a little. Oh, don't get me wrong, she's a good kid and I love her. But…"

"I totally understand," I said.

Ruby smiled a knowing look at me. "I suspect you do, dear. Well, most of the bedrooms are being remodeled and are a mess. Cousin Ed and his wife, Tula, will be in the room next to yours. The rest of my folks will be at the Rushmore Motel up on the highway." Her voice dropped to a whisper. "Tula has special needs, so she needs to stay close."

Aunt Angela piped up. "River and I will be glad to stay at the motel. I hate to put you to any inconvenience."

"Nonsense. It's been years since I've seen you. I want to visit with you. My folks will be fine at the motel. We had hoped the cabins at the lake would be ready to put guests in and one is, but mostly it's a mess out there. Weather delays, I guess. And most of the rooms here at the ranch are still being remodeled." Ruby blushed a deep pink. "I guess it was inconvenient of us to want to get married now before the ranch is ready and all, but neither of us wanted to wait. I wanted to be a June bride."

A mental picture flashed into my head of those two doing what it was that they no longer wanted to wait for and I winced a little. I felt an almost overwhelming need to scrub something.

"I usually stay over at Angus's place, but we hired a temporary nurse to stay with him for a while," Ruby continued. "I'm staying here. That way I can see to preparations for the wedding next week and take care of the needs of our houseguests. But, I'll look in on him every day. Colin put a hold on the construction until after the wedding. He's fixed himself a bed in the study off the kitchen here, so you can bunk with me in Colin's room, Angela. We'll get caught up."

Ruby grabbed my suitcase and started up the stairs, but I blocked her way and put my hand over hers. "Uh-uh," I said. She sighed and let go so I could tote my own luggage. I waved a goodbye to Mandy, leaving her washing vegetables. She gave me a two-eyed wink.

Ruby led me to Blair's room, although I knew the way. It looked exactly the same as when I used to play dollhouse with Blair, before Colin got so weird and I was not allowed to visit. Same lavender carpeting. Same red, green and purple poppy wallpaper. Stuffed bears positioned around the large room—one in a baby carriage and two nattily dressed ones at a small table with a tea set spread before them. There was no evidence of Blair ever getting past the age of five. Ruby's eyes scanned the room, making sure it was tidy, I guess, and left me.

"Holy crap, will Blair ever grow up?" I said out loud and fell back onto the ivory eyelet comforter on her queen bed. I landed next to a fat marmalade cat that I hadn't noticed, partially hidden under a pillow. He opened one eye, yawned, and pushed his paw onto my nose in a long stretch. "Do you think this room looks like it belongs to a girl street-smart enough to make it in New York City?" I asked, as I scratched the cat's ear.

Dogs barking outside caused the cat to right itself, back arched and hair on end. It hissed and jumped off the bed, then sprang through an open window.

I got up to get a better look. The window opened onto the roof of the room below. Not too far outside the window was a lawn chair by an empty soda pop can and an ashtray with one of Blair's thin cigarettes. A large tree bent its limb over the roof, offering shade. I wondered how many times Blair had snuck out of her room by climbing to the ground on that tree.

The room was in a wing on the east side of the ranch house, away from the pool area. This was the working side of the ranch. The view here was of barn and corrals, pastures and rutted dirt lanes. A few red hens scratched under a cottonwood tree. A decrepit flat trailer loaded down with hay leaned against one side of the barn. A lone pitchfork stuck up from the center of the hay like a candle on a birthday cake. The dogs had something cornered there and were barking a fuss. Maybe a skunk or raccoon, I guessed. Horses stood in paddocks, butt to head and head to butt, swishing their tails in each other's faces to keep flies away, unperturbed by the dogs.

I saw the barn doors open. A man leading a horse stepped out and the dogs scattered. Sunlight threw shadows across the horse's sleek, black coat. I smiled as I took in Darkwater's beauty. The tall man, wearing dusty denim pants and shirt, snakeskin boots and a black cowboy hat with a bright green band led the horse into a paddock. The horse reared up and I got the strangest sensation. It felt like fear, but not my fear.

For the briefest of moments, I saw a smoky cloud rise above the horse's head. In it was a picture of a knife and there was a meaty smell attached to it. This was such an unfamiliar sensation, I actually staggered and held onto the drapes. I tried to figure out what was going on. Was this a freaky sugar reaction brought on by Ruby's pies?

As soon as I asked myself the question, the answer intuitively came. Darkwater had seen this man use such a knife and was afraid because the man smelled like blood and meat. Okay. As freaky as this was, I'd go with it and try to figure it out.

For years, John had told me that he communicates with animals telepathically, long before anyone had heard the phrase *pet psychic*. I wasn't sure I believed him but he was my dad so I tried to cut him some slack. "Animals are easy to read," he once told me when he stopped by to visit on his way to Pow Wow in Oklahoma. "Not like two-leggeds. Animals communicate with images, and sometimes physical sensations." For John to know what an animal is thinking, he would study an image that would appear above the animal's head like a cartoon bubble.

When he explained this to me, I must have looked spooked. "John, I know you use peyote sometimes in shamanic ceremonies. Do you think maybe you've fried something in there?" I had asked, motioning at his noggin.

"Not a physical image," he had continued, ignoring my question. "It's something you see with spirit. Metaphysicians call it your third eye. You can do this, too, River. It's a gift that runs in our family. You can picture-talk back to the animal, too. All you have to do is think of a picture of what you want to say and mentally project it into the space slightly above your head. The animal will read your thought picture. Animals do it with each other all the time."

Uh-huh, sure. So, horses are herbivores, I reasoned. They don't initially trust people because we smell like the meat we eat. Maybe Darkwater thought he was going to be this man's dinner.

Darkwater acted out something awful, pulling on his lead and throwing his head back and snorting. I closed my eyes to stop the dizziness that threatened to make me bring up the pie. I looked again. All I saw was the man and horse. There was no cloud. There was no feeling of fear. No doubt about it. I was nuckin futz. I shook it off and continued to watch the man.

He appeared locked in a struggle of wills with the stallion. Putting up with no nonsense, he secured Darkwater's bottom lip in a twitch. A twitch is serious horse training dominance. It's a device that pinches the horse's lip like a clothespin if the horse jerks his head, and releases if the horse keeps his head still. Some trainers say it doesn't hurt, but my lips puckered in sympathy. After Darkwater stopped his bronco moves, the cowboy swung a saddle onto Darkwater's back, tightened the straps under the horse's belly and removed the twitch.

The stallion took off prancing, bucking and farting around the corral. After a while, he settled into a gallop. The man crooned soft words as he stood in the center of the paddock and kept the horse running in circles on a lunge. Throughout this performance, the cowboy slapped his leg to keep the horse moving. It was hypnotic. Eventually, the horse tired and his proud head came down and he licked his lips, coming to a stop. He turned and faced the cowboy. I knew from my long ago visits with John at the Rez that this was horse body language for "I give up." The man turned his back on Darkwater and walked around the corral. Darkwater followed him like a puppy.

I wasn't happy about the twitch. I had to admit, though, that the guy seemed to know his way around a horse. I turned to leave the window when the man removed his hat to wipe his forehead and looked up. The sunlight caught him full in the face. I gasped and jumped back, hoping he hadn't seen me. That silly Blair had neglected to tell me that the horse whisperer who was working with Darkwater was Billy Chance.

Stunned, I backed up. When I felt the back of my legs hit against the bed, they buckled and I fell backward onto the bed. Lying on my back, I squeezed my eyes shut and took some deep breaths. I had tried so hard to forget Billy's face. Now that face had morphed into this older, Leonardo DiCaprio version.

When I opened my eyes, that same face was now in the window, staring at me. Shimmying up that tree and onto this roof so fast had to have come from past experience crawling up here to see Blair. What a shit-for-brains cousin I had.

"Well, lookie here," he said as he lowered himself into the room, sat on the window ledge, and spit a toothpick onto the floor. "Long time no see, River Morning Star. I can't say I've missed you."

I didn't say anything. Just gave him a look that would've cut a diamond.

"Why don't you take your sorry tail right back to Kansas before it gets caught in a trap you can't get out of," he said.

I was suddenly eleven years old again, itching for a fight. I yearned to tear my nails into those eyes. I stood up, forcing my backbone to straighten. "Make me," I said.

In a few easy strides, he was across the room. I wanted to scream, but only a squeak escaped my lips before he bowled me over, back onto the bed. Billy swung one snakeskin boot across me and straddled me, his thighs effectively pinning my arms. His hand went over my mouth and a full-blown scream jumped from my belly and stuck in my throat.

"I couldn't believe my eyes when I saw you up here," he said. "But then I thought, what the hell? We need to have a little talk. It's time you and I got something straight."

I bit into his hand.

"Ouch, you little witch," he said, pulling his hand away. The opportunity to scream was there, but I made a conscious effort not to yield to it. I was not letting him think he intimidated me!

"You'll pay for that, just like you'll pay for the trouble I had after you accused me of killing your mother," he said, rubbing his hand. "My family's supposed friends! Hah! Some of them wouldn't give my mother the time of day after all your lies. It took a long time for Mom and Dad to hold their heads up again around here."

"Oh, poor you," I said. "You and your family lost some friends, did you? Well, I lost my mother. You murdered her! Now get off me and go back off in your own jack yard, you big lummox." I wiggled under him.

His thighs tightened around my arms. "You know, River, I'm so tired of your crap. I didn't murder anybody. If you think you're going to make trouble for me again, you'd be sorely mistaken. I have plans now. If you try to screw up my life again you little liar I will take you out. I'm not talking about on a date." I struggled to move against him, but he felt like a refrigerator.

"Don't bother telling Colin about this," he said. "He wouldn't walk across the street for the likes of you."

Looking in his eyes made me dizzy, or was it the lack of oxygen from his body smashing my lungs? I spit in his face. I thought he was pulling his hand back to strike me, but instead he scooped his hand under my neck and pulled my face so close to his face I could feel his breath on my cheek. Then, he put his tongue on my chin and drew it all the way up to my forehead in one big slurp. It felt like a trail of snail snot.

"Jesus!" I said. Hot tears sprang to my eyes. I felt myself blush red-hot from my toes to the top of my head.

"I mean it," he said. "You do not want to mess with me. I saw you watching me with Darkwater. Did you see how he became mine? Before I'm through with him, he'll be coming to me when I call and stopping on a whistle. I'm talking total domination. You hear? Mess with me, and I will dominate you, too."

Was he threatening to rape me? Sounding braver than I felt, I said, "Oh, you're so full of shit. Get over yourself, will you?" I wiggled under him. "Get off me!"

The cat jumped back into the room from the window sill, hitting the floor with a thud. The distraction caused Billy to look, turning his body just enough to offer me a window of opportunity. I gave my knee a quick upward jerk between his legs. He doubled over and rolled off me with a groan. When he pulled himself halfway up and headed toward the window, I pushed my foot into his butt, sending him sprawling across the floor. I was up in a shot and grabbed a letter opener from the nightstand, slashing the air between us. "Dominate this, asshole!" I shouted.

I heard Blair coming down the hall toward the bedroom, singing her lungs out. Billy limped to the window and crawled out onto the porch roof. With a backward glance, he grabbed onto the tree limb. "You just wait. When you're not looking, pow." He smashed his fist into his other palm, letting go of the limb and losing his balance in the effort. I heard him hit the ground. A few muffled curse words floated up.

Blair stuck her head into the room and pulled an earpiece from her ear. "I live to rap," she said.

I'm standing there with the letter opener in my hand. My reflection in the mirror shows me that my hair looks like it's been in a hurricane. Shows me a blouse that used to be ironed now wrinkled and unbuttoned. Shows me teary eyes. Blair may not have heard anything because of the music, but did she not see these things?

Totally oblivious, she popped the earpiece back in and continued dancing to a song I couldn't hear. I walked to her and pulled it out of her ear. "Blair, why didn't you tell me Billy was the horse trainer?"

"What the…you saw Billy? Jeez, River. I'm sorry. I told him we were having guests. He promised me he'd stay invisible today."

"He so lied," I said.

She flipped her hair back over her shoulder. I sensed she was stalling because she couldn't give me a good explanation for omitting that information. "Well, bummer, huh?" she said. "But now the ice has been broken between you two. I assume you didn't kill him, as you feared you might."

That was true. He had upset me. He had scared me so bad my panty crotch was wet. But I hadn't killed Billy, even though with that letter opener I could have. I could've shoved his nose cartilage back into his brain or poked my fingers into his eyes like I'd seen in some of Aunt Angela's self-defense videos. I hadn't done that. Maybe I didn't have murder in me. Or maybe it was just my common sense telling me that I'd have a gnat's chance if I killed the sheriff's son. But I could and did hurt him. That thought made me feel all fuzzy and warm inside.

I guess Blair didn't consider the incident worth further conversation because she danced over to the closet and pulled out a turquoise silk blouse and cream silk pants. She tossed them on the bed. "These are my fat clothes. Here, try on. The blouse matches perfectly those earrings you have on. In fact, wear anything in this closet that you like. If I'm going to introduce you around as my cousin, you'll need to wear something better than those rags you brought. I have an image to maintain, after all."

"Fat clothes?"

"Oh, I guess I didn't tell you. I gained a few pounds after you left Pell Mell. Lost it but I couldn't make myself get rid of these clothes. You're what? Size twelve? I think that's what these are. It's not fair. Tall people can eat anything and not put on the pounds."

She popped the earpiece back in her ear and sailed from the room like an ice skater on speed. I wanted to tell her about Billy's attack but I was talking to air. She probably wouldn't have believed me. Or, knowing her, she had arranged it. I knew I wouldn't report it. Who was I going to tell? The sheriff, who happened to be Billy's dad? Billy was probably right about Colin not being able to stand me. Telling him would do me no good. Aunt Angela and Ruby were having such a good time. I hated to spoil their reunion.

As usual, I sucked it up.

I picked up Blair's blouse and held it against me in front of the mirror. Not bad. I had never considered myself fat. I guess a size twelve compared to Blair's size five might seem fat to her. I was a foot taller and that made all the difference. The pants were another story; much too short. I picked out a skirt in some swishy turquoise and beige fabric that I thought would work, and tossed it on the bed with the blouse.

I engaged the door lock and closed and locked the window on the way to the bathroom down the hall where steaming hot water and lavender scented shower gel washed the smell of Billy off me. I scrubbed down the shower with spray cleaner I found under the sink to keep it nice for Tula and Earl. I made sure the towels were all lined up the same way and the toilet paper roll fell over instead of under and folded it into a little triangle at the end.

I pulled on my robe and went back to Blair's room and slipped on the blouse and skirt. I tied my hair back with an abalone shell clasp. I sat on the bed and slid my feet into my transparent jelly sandals. I got them at Wal-Mart for $3.99, but they still looked good with the expensive outfit. I hadn't realized how good it would feel to wear silk instead of denim. "Wear anything of hers I like, huh?" I said to the cat. "Well, if she says so. I'll wear the fibers right out on these beautiful clothes. That's the least she can do for me after that fiasco with Billy." My eyes threatened to fill up, but I shook it off. I would not give that creep power over me.

The cat jumped onto my lap. "Oh, no you don't," I said, as I stood up. "I'll have a cat hair overcoat if you stay there." The cat looked up, assessed me with her slanted eyes as she landed on the floor. I picked her up, being careful not to hold her close and placed her on the bed. I felt around in my purse and pulled out a little thimble-sized cream container that came with the coffee on the airplane. I peeled off the top and held it out for her. As her rough tongue scooped up the creamy treat, I was thinking about how she had saved me from Billy with her distraction. "Thank you," I said as I scratched her ear.

A small cloud formed over her head. In it was a picture of her licking my hand. A gesture of thanks? I shivered and turned to go, calling the cat out of the bedroom. I didn't look at her as I closed the bedroom door and headed down to the party.

Chapter Seven

"Isn't he a dear?" said the large woman approaching me, motioning to the little boy standing on a makeshift bandstand by the pool. "We call him Little Elvis." She sat down on two folding metal chairs beside me and introduced herself as Ruby's cousin, Tula. The little boy, Ruby's six-year-old nephew in full Elvis costume, was belting out, "Love Me Tender" on the karaoke mike. I pulled the chicken liver, water chestnut and bacon appetizer off the toothpick with my teeth and tossed the toothpick back on the plate. "Very talented," I said.

Ruby and Colin's party had been going on since late afternoon, and everyone seemed to be enjoying it. Ruby's family, as promised by Blair, was a true mix of fruits and nuts and I had liked every one of them. I'd met uncles and aunts, cousins, cousins twice removed and steps, and they all seemed sweet and unpretentious with a little bit of redneck mixed in.

The day was waning and patio lights were coming on. Warming trays that had been set up on tables underneath the awning now held the remnants of the dinner Ruby had spent all day preparing. People milled around the trays, enjoying the rich fragrance of the remaining barbequed meat, drinking and laughing. Cousin Tula's plate held only green beans, watercress salad and two olives.

I had met Earl, Tula's husband, earlier and I now knew all about Tula. Totally unprovoked, he had explained to me that Tula weighed over three hundred pounds due to an eating disorder that caused her to eat while sleepwalking. I hadn't asked. But he, like everybody in Ruby's family, seemed to want to share personal information.

"Her doctor over in Pierre says it would be dangerous to wake her while she's having an episode," Earl had said as he maneuvered me around a wooden dancing platform. "I've tried locking her in the bedroom, locking up the refrigerator. She just ends up trashing everything if she can't get to the food. She's tried sedatives, but she hates that drugged out feeling she has in the morning. So the doctor has been giving her hypnosis treatments. Says that'll cure her eventually."

Those treatments had begun two years ago, during which time Earl had been plunking down two hundred dollars per session for his beloved's weekly therapy. It appeared that Tula wasn't the only one being fed a load of crap.

Tula picked up a lone olive, looked at it like she resented it for not being steak, and popped it into her mouth. "I'm sure if I could just get a handle on this sleepwalking thing," she said, "I could be as skinny as…oh, say, that girl over there."

I followed her nod to a tall slender brunette in a black sheath dress. Over six feet tall with runner's legs all the way to her butt and a nicely contoured back suggesting the girl worked out, she was someone people noticed, even with the little lines around her mouth that said she was the other side of forty. She saw us looking at her, and walked over. Smiling, she extended her hand to me. She said, in a southern accent, "You know, I've been standing over there thinking and thinking about who you might be. You wouldn't be Briana Morning Star's sweet little girl, would you?"

Had I ever been considered sweet? In Blair's silk blouse with my freshly polished nails and Chanel perfume that I found on Blair's dresser, I felt sweet indeed. "I don't know about the sweet part, but I'm River," I said, and held out my hand.

"Samantha Peet," she said. "You may not remember me. I used to substitute teach occasionally for your dear mother at Pell Mell Elementary. Such a sweet lady. Even though I live in Memphis now, I still keep in touch with people at the school. They all still miss her."

Samantha Peet and Clive Bilby. Although the faces had been a blur, those were two names I would never forget. They were the witnesses to my mother's murder. They had seen Billy push my mother that day, but for some reason they had not seen it like I had. My hand went limp in hers.

"Thank you," I said. "Memphis, huh?"

"Yes. Wonderful city, Memphis. But it's nice to be back to see old friends. When I got the invitation, I was afraid my boss wouldn't give me the time off, but the silly old thing did. I'm working for a lawyer there." She cleared her throat. "I just loved the kids at school," she said as she stabbed an olive with a toothpick, "but this opportunity came along back home and I couldn't pass it up. I had some legal aide experience, so away I went. As you may know, teachers in Pell Mell don't make much money. But I do still miss my favorite students. Blair was one, so I guess that's how I ended up being invited."

"Ms. Peet," I said, "do you still talk to Clive?"

"Clive? Clive Bilby, the bus driver?" A look of recognition spread across her face. "Oh, you remember us as witnesses to that terrible tragedy." She shook her head. "I sure am sorry that we couldn't back you up on the story you told. But, frankly, I just didn't see what you did. Anyway, tragedy comes to all of us in our turn, I guess. I heard that Clive died in a house fire."

A voice came from behind us. "Yes, a terrible shame. Clive was a respected man. His funeral was well attended." I turned. Billy's mother, Reverend Ardis Chance, stood before me, her large hands folded together against the front of her black pleated skirt. A large silver crucifix hung on a chain against her chest. I could've cut myself on the crease in the sleeves of her tailored shirtwaist white blouse. Fifty-something, I guessed. Her curly, steel gray hair was cropped close to her scalp. It appeared that if I reached up and pulled at a lock of it, it would pop back like a tight spring. Silver wire frames with lavender-tinted lens hung on a nose that, oddly, tracked slightly to the right. I smiled. Maybe she'd broken it in a bar fight. A wild white hair sprung from a place just under her chin.

"Reverend Chance, how nice to see you," said Samantha. "You know River, of course."

"Of course," she said, and extended her long fingers, bending slightly at the waist. I gave her hand a slight pump. Blair had told me Ardis would be the preacher who was marrying Ruby and Colin, so I had known I would see her in the pulpit at the wedding. But I hadn't wanted to talk to her. She and I hadn't had a pleasant time when I accused her son of murder years ago.

She looked at me a long moment. "I didn't think you'd come. Thought I'd never see you again, truth to tell. But here you are," she said with breath that smelled of liquor. "I've waited a long time..." she said, and then seemed to notice Samantha's frown. "Oh, I mean, I'm gratified that even though Ruby and Colin won't be attending my church, Colin still wanted me to do their wedding." She leaned toward me. "Ruby belongs to some fundamentalist sect, you know. I believe he'll be attending church."

Her voice had the same pleasant radio announcer voice I remembered from my mother's funeral when she, among others, had given me her regrets. I believe that was the week before she called me a lying Jezebel and told me I was going to hell for telling authorities I had seen Billy force my mother over the cliff edge.

"I certainly hope you have healed from your past trials in this town," she said, slurring her words a bit. "I know my son hopes that, too. It's so hard when you're young to lose your mother like that. It makes your mind play tricks." When I didn't respond, she continued, "Well, in the past now. I almost didn't recognize you. You've grown into a beautiful young woman." She looked me up and down. "Hasn't she, Samantha?"

"Much like your mother," said Samantha. "You have her eyes. I see your father too, in your hair and the way you stand.

How is your father?"

"Okay, I guess. I haven't seen him for a few months. I hope to get out to the Rez soon. Maybe attend one of his shamanic healing ceremonies."

Ardis cut me a sideways look. "I hope you haven't taken up any of your father's ways, believing that animals and stones have souls and such?"

Did I have a sign on my back? One that said, "Tell me what to think." I had not been talking to Ardis for five minutes and she was telling me what to believe. I was about to be rude and I felt incapable of stopping myself. I heard the testiness in my own voice.

"My father is Lakota," I said. "He has a history, Reverend Chance. His history is that his people were forced to give up their land and live on reservations. They were not allowed to wear their traditional clothing." I think my hands went to my hips at this point. "They were not allowed to dance or celebrate their traditional ceremonies. The children were beaten if they spoke the Lakota language." I spread my hands, palms up, in a placating gesture. "It wasn't until nineteen seventy-eight that Lakota religious practices became legal and attempts to eradicate a whole culture ceased. Since we are now in the twenty-first century and it's mandated by law, can't you at least leave him his religion?"

Ardis stepped back like I had slapped her. "That is not religion! That's hocus-pocus! Do you think it's all right to worship a white buffalo? Do you think the earth is your mother? You may be half-Indian, River, but you don't have to buy into that."

Being Indian wasn't something I'd thought a lot about since leaving South Dakota. But the little time I had spent with John at the Rez when I was a kid had brought me an appreciation of the ways of the Old Ones. John had a right to his beliefs. This lady was ticking me off.

"Well," I said, "in a very real sense, the earth is our mother. We come from her and in the end, she claims us. I mean, without the earth, we wouldn't even be here, would we?"

"Oh, for heaven's sake!" she said. "Of all the—"

Samantha spoke up. "Reverend Chance, I'm sure you don't want to ruin this lovely party for yourself and others with this debate."

Ardis made a couple throat clearing sounds. "You're right, of course. I have forgotten myself. I'm just so distressed lately at the way the young people of this country are going down the drain. Have you heard about the Satanic worshippers in our own community? Colin was telling me about the ritualistic killing of his cattle. I'll bet it's teenagers. I mean adults wouldn't do such a thing. Some of those kids involved must be kids we know." She shook her head. "It's those books they can get on the Internet nowadays. All about magic and getting in touch with spirit guides and talking to dead people."

"Don't worry about me on that score," I said. "The last thing I want is someone else, dead or alive, trying to tell me how to live and—"

"Well, thank you for your views, River," Ardis cut me off. "Be sure and come to services before you leave town. As the Good Book says, 'Forsake not the assembling of yourselves together.'" She turned on her heel and left.

"Let us not forget that alcohol kills brain cells," I said under my breath. When I realized Samantha had heard me, we both laughed. I stuffed a crab cake in my mouth, hoping if I kept it full I might keep myself from getting into trouble.

"I guess we ought to cut her a break," Samantha said. "Ardis is under a lot of stress these days, what with Billy getting married to some retarded girl."

I felt a sinking sensation move into my belly. "Getting married to...?" I said.

"Oh, my goodness," she said, and covered her mouth briefly with her hand. "Mandy is your sister. I had forgotten. Then, surely you know about the wedding?"

"No. No, I didn't."

"Well, sweetie, sorry you had to hear it like this. I know you have a history with Billy. It can't be easy to hear he's going to be your brother-in-law."

I swallowed hard and sat down as Samantha made her way around the pool to talk to other guests.

"I ought to give her a face full of fingernails," said Blair, sitting down beside me, stunning in something sheer and flowery with a matching shoulder wrap.

"Who? Samantha?"

"No. Your stupid sister. She's over there, flashing a diamond ring around, claiming Billy gave it to her."

"Is it true?" I asked.

"Of course it's not true," she said. "Mandy lives in some la-la land in her head. Billy would never marry her, unless he's..."

I gasped. "He's the baby's father, isn't he? I swear if he raped her, I'll ..."

"No, he's not the baby's father! I was going to say unless he's trying to get me jealous."

Well, of course. Blair would think this whole thing was about her. "He's not interested in you, Blair," I said. "If he were, he'd be over here with you and not walking over to put his arm around Mandy."

She followed my nod. Billy had moved to Mandy's side. He must've felt the heat coming from Blair's eyes because he turned toward us. When he saw her glaring at him, he went as erect and stiff as a tongue depressor, his lips in a thin line.

Blair flew out of her chair, marched around the pool, and grabbed Mandy by the arm. Mandy smiled, and flashed her ring for Blair to see. Billy moved to stand between them.

I couldn't hear what Blair was saying over the music, but I surmised from my lipreading skills that every other word rhymed with duck. I was pretty sure it wasn't a conversation about water fowl, though. Mandy seemed to take it in stride. She may not understand everything, but she understood that she had one-upped Blair.

Blair stomped back to me and sat down. Tears trickled down her cheeks. "It's true, then?" I asked, and she nodded.

"Jesus. That boy could open his own franchise of Nightmares R Us," I said.

"It's not his fault," Blair said. "It's her. Her and her ho ways. If it weren't for her, he'd love me. She's such a whore she even seduced my dad. That's his baby she's carrying."

At first I laughed. In a sadistic way, it was funny to see Blair finally want something that she couldn't have. But when I saw the depressed look in her eyes, I softened toward her. "You can't know that," I said.

"Believe me, I know. It's gross. I caught them in the act. It happened before Ruby, when Daddy was dealing with Grandpa Angus on his own." She wiped her tears on the heel of her hand. "Oh, I probably shouldn't be telling you any of this."

Colin was the baby's father? Oh, be still my squeamish stomach. "That's crazy," I said. "He must be what, forty-something? I know they're not related by blood, but he's her step-uncle, for crying out loud."

She put her head in her hands and sobbed. I put my arm around her shoulders and said, "Tell me." I had the same presentiment of doom I had the day she talked me into touching an electric fence when we were kids.

Blair picked up a napkin and blotted her eyes. "It started when Grandpa got too dimwitted to take care of himself. He insisted that only Daddy take care of him, but he wouldn't leave his house. Daddy wanted to bring Grandpa here to live but Grandpa wouldn't have it. There wasn't enough time in the day to take care of Grandpa at his place and get this guest ranch operation off the ground. Daddy was constantly worried. He'd never gone head-to-head with Grandpa before. I guess he went through some kind of breakdown. He'd belt back a few, you know, to get to sleep. Then he got to drinking so much he was losing chunks of time. He went on a bender and blacked out a couple days, leaving Grandpa totally on his own. He doesn't remember a thing, including banging Mandy, to this day. And I'll never tell him."

She tossed the damp napkin onto the table. "I guess blacking out scared him, because he quit booze cold turkey after that and told Grandpa he was getting a nurse and he could accept that or die in a nursing home. It was about a week later that he hired Ruby."

I digested all that for a minute. "Just because they may have screwed once doesn't mean the baby is Colin's," I said, hoping, hoping it wasn't true.

"Whose baby would it be? Her foster brothers have been

out of her life for a while now and Billy was in Arkansas all that fall on some kind of rodeo circuit. He was gone about four months, so I know he didn't get her pregnant. He's the only guy, besides her brothers, I've ever seen around Mandy. No other guy was even nice to her. It's Daddy's all right. Why couldn't he have just blacked out before they did the deed?"

Can anyone give me an amen? I thought, as I pulled Blair's wrap up around her shoulders. If Colin had been driving drunk, and blacked out and killed someone, then that would be manslaughter. There should be equivalent jail time for having a drunken accident with a penis.

Blair picked up a glass of amber liquid someone had left on a table and belted it down. "Mandy's the one I blame," she said.

I recalled an animated movie that Mom had shown Mandy, along with our fourth grade class about how babies are made, with some information in the mix about venereal disease in case anyone thought it sounded like fun. Mandy had thought the baby thing was the biggest whopper she'd ever heard. Her belief that God sent a seed to a woman's tummy while asleep made more sense to her. I doubt she connected what she and Colin did to creating a human life. She probably just knew it felt good and it made Colin happy. She, like Colin, probably didn't even remember it.

"Blair, you have to tell Colin the baby is his," I said.

"No. Religious as Ruby is, if she finds out Daddy and Mandy are having a baby together, she'll back out of the marriage. I can just hear her saying something stupid like that in the eyes of God Mandy and Daddy are already married because they're having a child together or some nonsense like that. She'll take her fine managerial skills with her. Daddy will go into a deep dark place and be too hard to live with. And that'll be the end of any hope I have of ever leaving here. It will end badly for everyone. You have to promise me you won't tell Daddy."

She sat up straight. "Ohmigod! What if the baby looks just like Daddy? What if Daddy looks at that kid and remembers? Or what if Ruby recognizes Daddy in that child? That kid could be a living time bomb. You've got to talk Mandy out of marrying Billy and going back to that shelter of yours. Get her out of state. C'mon, River. You've just got to."

I didn't want to. I wanted to leave this place and its problematic people. But I thought about Mandy's baby and how I loved her and how she'd probably forget that baby someday in a women's restroom somewhere or leave it in a bathtub full of water by itself. Or, it would get put in foster care like I did.

Shit and Doom. I once again saw myself standing by Blair and reaching for that electric fence.

Chapter Eight

The next morning brought a new edition of the Pell Mell *Star*, which I scanned as I sat by the pool in robe and pajamas drinking orange juice and eating a bear claw. A corporate executive had embezzled someone's 401k. An athlete was on steroids. Some terrorists were caught plotting. Same stuff. Different day.

Party debris was everywhere. I kicked a plastic cup out from under my chair. Pink crepe paper streamers floated on the water in the pool. A busted yellow and pink piñata hung from a tree branch. The pink-striped awning, half torn down, kept the sun from hitting me in the eyes. A few barn cats were busy on the tables licking plates. I had Ruby figured for a 'can't go to bed unless it's all in order' person, but I guess I was wrong. She could tie one on with the best of them. Here was the proof. Hurricane Ruby aftermath.

Mandy stood by the pool, holding a swimming pool skimmer with a long handle. She seemed to enjoy dipping it in the water and retrieving cups, streamers and other debris.

"Is that fun?" I asked, smiling at her.

"Oh, yes." Her eyes sparkled and I realized that with her childlike mind, every activity became a game and every day a new adventure. One of God's little compensations.

"Mandy, can we talk?" I asked and patted the chair by me.

She put the skimmer down. "I guess Ruby won't mind if I take a little break," she said. She sat by me and took a big bite of my roll, shoving the food into her cheeks. She pushed her front teeth out and made rodent noises at me.

"Mouse?" I asked.

"No, rabbit," she said. "I guess I'll have to work on that one."

"Yes, you will," I said, and gave her swollen body a hug. "I'm glad you're my sister."

I remembered how she'd looked before I left Pell Mell. John had been sober for a year, so social services had let him take us on a rare outing. He took us to Pow Wow on the Rez. We ate Indian tacos and watched the cowboys bite the dust at the rodeo. Mandy wore a Native American costume called a jingle dress. She danced during intermission, the little silver cones on her costume dress bouncing and jiggling to the drumbeat. It was our last good time together. Now she was here, fat with this baby.

"I'm glad you're my sister, too," she said.

"And," I said, hoping I wasn't about to make her mad. "I'm glad you're having this beautiful baby, but I worry about how you will care for it." She shuffled her legs under her chair and her smile faltered. I patted her knee.

"I know you used to forget to feed Iguana Jo in my mom's classroom," I said. "You can't forget to feed a baby." I shook my head as I said this and she did, too. "And, remember how you used to get mad and throw your baby doll against the wall? You can't throw a real baby."

She creased her forehead in thought. "Sometimes I don't want the stupid baby. Other times, I can't wait to kiss it and kiss it. I am, you know, up and down."

"Yes, I know," I said.

She pushed her hair behind her ear. "I know I am... you know, special. But, I do know how to care for babies. I know you can't throw them. I know you have to feed them and change their diapers. You spank them only if they are very, very bad."

"What do you think is bad?" I asked.

"I don't know. Billy will help me decide what is bad for the baby. He says he'll take care of this baby, too."

I swallowed the lump in my throat. "Mandy, do you love Billy? Do you want to live with him forever and ever?"

"Sometimes he doesn't want me around and he gets mad at me and yells. But he gave me this beautiful ring, so he must love me. I can't blame him. Most people get mad and yell at me. He never hits. Not like his momma hit him. She locked him in a dark closet once."

Billy, abused? He deserved every slap his mother gave him. "You're right," I said. "People shouldn't hit their children or put them in closets. I know some nice people who would love your baby so much if you would let them raise it." I patted her hand. "They would never hurt it. They have lots of money to buy the things it will need."

"Babies need lots of things," she said, thoughtfully.

"Yes, they do. These people would love you, too, for giving them your baby. Come back with me to Aunt Angela's house in Kansas. Let us find a good, safe place for your baby to live and good parents that love it. You can stay with us as long as you want. I'll make you some of those brownies you love."

She looked thoughtful. Then she looked at me and put her nose in the air like she smelled sour milk. "Billy said you might try to talk me into giving you my baby. Not gonna work. I'm keeping my baby. God planted it so He must think I can take care of it. And I am marrying Billy. Babies need fathers. Not like the one we had, but a better one, like Billy. I do love you, River, but don't talk to me about this ever again." She got up and went back to her pool cleaning.

I sighed and looked up to see Blair approaching, a look of resignation on her face. She jangled car keys in front of me and dropped them onto the paper, tearing it in half. "Well, I guess I'm locked in for the day," she said.

She looked balefully toward Mandy. "I don't know why she can't do this cleanup by herself. Or, if Ruby thinks it's too much for Mandy, you'd think she and Daddy could spend a few bucks and have it professionally done. Daddy used to give me money all the time, but Ruby's given him some load of crap about how I'm spoiled. I swear, if I didn't need her to make Daddy…" She put her hands on her hips and drop kicked a paper cup. "Making me help with cleanup is messed up." Her eyes had the confused look of a first-year trig student. I liked Ruby more and more all the time.

"Well, you might as well take the key to my 'Stang," she said, resignation in her voice. "I know you want to see your dad. Ride out to the Rez. Maybe you two can conjure a hex to make Mandy leave with you and Aunt Angela." Mandy looked over at us, smiled, and scratched her nose with her middle finger.

I glanced around. "I doubt I'll be taking the car anywhere today." I rubbed my eyes. They felt like they'd been dipped in sand. I was tired. Still, I felt I should help with cleanup for the party from the night before. It might even cheer me up to clean. Making things tidy and shiny usually did. I picked up an ashtray and tossed it into a nearby can.

"Put that down," Ruby shouted through the kitchen window, sounding like a good imitation of General Patton. I could hear garbage disposal sounds coming from the kitchen as she said, "I'm ashamed I didn't get to this clean up after the party last night. Too much carrying on, I guess. You're a guest and I won't allow you to help. Blair, however, has no such amnesty." Blair let out a sigh and rolled her eyes so far back into her head I thought she was having a seizure.

"I heard that," Ruby yelled.

I figured I'd better go before Ruby changed her mind. I left Ruby and Blair arguing over who would load the dishwasher and who would sweep the patio and Mandy serenely dipping her wand into the pool. I headed up to Blair's room and changed into an Old Navy T-shirt, jeans and tennis shoes, then headed back downstairs. Blair gave me a last longing look over her shoulder as I crossed the patio and made my way to her car.

I walked past the barn and corrals on my way to the detached five-car garage. Billy had Darkwater on a lunge, running him in circles in the corral. I meant to walk past him like he was under Harry Potter's invisible cloak, my nose in the air. He saw me and slowed Darkwater to a halt. He pulled his finger across his throat, then pointed at me. I countered by circling my thumb and index finger together and shoving my other index finger back and forth through it a few times. He then put his hand on his crotch and thrust his pelvis at me. I licked my fingers, slapped my ass, and blew him a kiss. When his complexion took on a purple hue, I figured my work was done. I double-timed it to the garage.

I clicked the garage door opener on Blair's keychain. My prize was behind door number four. I scurried over to the Mustang and lowered myself onto the buttery soft leather. It formed itself around my derriere like it had personal knowledge of my butt and I slowed down to savor the feel. My fingertips tingled as I touched the steering wheel and gently eased the hot car out of the garage. I saw Billy in the rearview mirror, heading toward me, a look of resolve on his face. I hit the gas and pulled out of the gravel drive onto Interstate 44 doing eighty, heading out to Pine Ridge Reservation.

Chapter Nine

I headed down Highway 44 East. Ahead of me loomed the jagged moonscape of Badlands National Park. Jutting out of the flatland prairie and pockmarked with craters and jagged rock formations, the Badlands looked like pictures I had seen of the moon.

As I turned onto BIA 27 and headed to Scenic, the dusty town near where John lived, a man walking alongside the road with a stick and a big plastic sack waved to me, then bent over to retrieve an empty can. His dog peed on the sagebrush that grew in patches here and there. A small boy on a motor scooter stirred up dust as he drove through the open door of a building decorated with geometric Native American patterns in red, yellow, black and white. *Cigarettes Here* blinked from a neon sign in the window. The kid came back out the door, again riding on the scooter, but this time toting a six-pack of beer.

I made a right turn onto a blacktop road that took me past a hodgepodge of government housing, some tidy and some in various stages of falling apart. When the blacktop ended, the 'Stang bucked and bumped along hard ruts on a dried gumbo road that led to John's place, an old farmhouse that had been in his family for years.

When the road curved, I could see John's dirt yard surrounded by a broken rock fence. I pulled up to the fence and got out of the car, looking up at the vast sky full of clouds marching in front of the sun so that sunshine graced the dusty, tumbleweed-covered land in fits and starts. I should have been looking where my feet were going. Dog crap stuck to the bottom of my shoe. Figured. I pulled my shoe off and got busy scraping it across a rock while I looked around.

I noticed two examples of creative housing to either side of John's yard. A plywood entry had been tacked onto a dilapidated train car. Discarded beer cans marked the space around the train car and an outhouse leaned precariously in the back. Next door to that was a dwelling made of various wood packing crates and large appliance boxes, reinforced by old tires and corrugated tin. Two old jalopies rested on cinder blocks.

By comparison with his neighbors, John's rickety farmhouse was a castle. The screen door was busted through, but the windows seemed okay, and the bright blue paint looked fresh. The porch sagged but didn't give way when I stood on it. A skinny yellow dog skulked across the dirt yard. Large ticks hung from its body like jewels from the neck of a society matron. Out of the corner of my eye, movement stirred.

"Hello, Uncle Charley." I smiled at the old man as he came around the corner of the house. Charley is not my uncle, but I had learned as a child on the Rez to always address my elders this way, as a sign of respect. He looked the same now as he did when I was five. Old as dirt.

"My, my. You're a sight for sore eyes," Charley said, his face wrinkling into a smile. His skin had the texture of an old apple left out in the sun. "Last time I saw you, you were running across this yard, chasing a green snake with a stick."

"I still like to chase snakes," I said.

"Watch they don't chase you," he said. "There are a few of the two-legged variety around here that would like to catch a juicy little mouse like you." He leaned his shoulder into mine. "Here comes one now," he whispered. His voice got louder as a young woman approached. "These young Lakota," Charley said, "riding around here in their cars, playing loud music, looking for no good. They should be walking the Good Red Road, not fooling around where they don't belong." I had seldom heard Charlie say more than one sentence. Never a whole paragraph.

A tall, lean girl the color of a mocha latte stepped onto the porch, holding a sandwich in one hand and a soda in the other. She wore a thin white T-shirt splattered with paint splotches. Her sleeves were rolled up over biceps that looked like Linda Hamilton's in the first *Terminator* movie. Faded denim pants stretched tight across her thighs, ragged at the bottoms. Her kneecaps showed through ripped threads. She had the dark hair of the Lakota, but with big blond chunks here and there, cut into a bushy gelled spiky 'do. The whole effect was so just got out of bed, I had to smile. She pushed back a chunk of dyed honey-blond hair that had fallen onto her forehead and locked onto me with brown sugar eyes and a thousand-watt smile.

"Old man, what are you saying?" She put her arm around Charley. "You know you were just as bad at nineteen as I am."

"Probably worse." Charley spit tobacco over the railing. "But you are my granddaughter, Toni Thunderheart. I expected more of you." Uncle Charley turned to me. "If your dad isn't in the house, he may be out back in the barn." He dismissed us both, and walked away. "Good to see you," he said as he moved off the porch.

"You, too, Uncle."

"Watch out for snakes," Charley said over his shoulder. "Especially that one you're standing next to."

I stepped back from Toni. "He's sure down on you," I said. "By the way, I'm River. John is my father."

"Very nice to meet you," Toni said, extending her hand. I noticed she wore no rings and her fingernails were nubs. A nicotine stain showed on the middle finger of her left hand. "Don't mind him. He and me just got a difference of opinion on how I should live my life. You know how it is when other people want to live your life for you and you won't let 'em. They get testy."

Boy, did I ever. "Nothing serious, I hope."

"Well, nothing unexpected. Grandpa and my parents believe if you're over eighteen, and not going to school, you need to get out and work for a living. You know, get on at the plant or get a paycheck from the mall, not do what I do."

"Are you doing what you do here on the Rez?"

"Well, yes and no," she said as I banged on John's door. "I never got the chance, as a kid, to see this place. My dad left the Rez when he was young, joined the army and married Mom. Never came back. I thought it was time to visit the roots, so to speak, so I hitched out from Minnesota. Grandpa about had a coronary when I showed up. Hitching and all, he said it was dangerous. But he could hardly turn me away since I'd made such an effort to get here. He had no room at his place, which it turns out is just a cabover camper sitting on the ground, so John took me in as a favor to him."

I stepped off the porch and made my way around the house to the barn. Toni followed. "Holy cow," I said, as I rounded the corner. A mural in bright fuchsia, tan, gold and purple graced one whole side of John's barn. It was of two eagles in flight, claws and beaks extended, hurtling toward each other against a backdrop of canyons.

"I did that," said Toni, obviously pleased with herself.

I was impressed. "Pretty good," I said.

"Just pretty good?"

"Okay, better than pretty good."

Toni smiled that smile at me again. "Your dad said I wasn't good for much of anything around here, so he told me to come up with something to keep myself busy. So, I painted the house. Then I did this. This is the stuff I mentioned that I want to do for a living but that my parents think is crap." She cleared her throat. "You know, eagles only mate during flight as they free-fall toward the ground. These two are streaking toward major foreplay."

"So, you've painted a nasty poultry picture. Can porn be far behind?" I blushed when I realized I was flirting. I turned away from her and plowed through the weeds to the barn. She fell into rhythm beside me.

"Maybe we could get together sometime, have a beer?" she asked, as grasshoppers jumped against our denim-covered legs like hot popcorn.

"I can't do beer."

"How about a little weed then?"

"Nope."

"Shit, girl. What can I do with you for a good time? Here's my number, anyway." She pulled out a stubby pencil and piece of paper from her back pocket, wrote on it, and shoved it into my jeans pocket. "We'll put out heads together, see if we can think of something." I watched her buns as she walked to John's back door. She turned to look at me, put her thumb to her ear with her little finger pointing to her lips in the universal "call me" sign.

Except for Toni's colorful addition, the weathered gray barn hadn't changed since before Mom and Dad split. One hinge kept the loft door in place. Several barn cats stayed busy, washing their feet and backs, their eyes nearly shut with pleasure. As I stepped across the threshold, the sweet smell of hay and horse dung filled my nose. It reminded me of good times, with the horses and my father, before the whiskey years.

I didn't see John, so I walked through the barn and out the other end to the pasture. I found him leaning over a very pregnant mare where she lay on the ground. The horse had long gashes running above her shoulder and down her flank and John was covered in her blood.

"Toni," he said, not looking up. "She's in a bad way. Bobcat, maybe a cougar. Come around here and hold this mare's head."

Seeing so much blood made my voice quiver. "It's uh, me, River," I said.

He looked up, worry in his eyes, but gave me a smile. "Rainbow Warrior Woman," he said, using my Indian name. "Get down here and hold her head while I stop the bleeding."

I kneeled in the dirt to steady the mare's head. When I touched her, pain tore through me. The sensation shocked me so hard I nearly tipped sideways. "She's not going to make it," I said. Her pain continued to course through me as John pressed his hands into the wound to staunch the flow of blood that was getting on both of us. Finally, she ceased her labored breathing. Relieved, I took a deep breath. I knew she was gone.

"There's her colt to think of now. It's a long shot, but she's at term." John stood up and pulled a knife from his boot. He slid the knife across the mare's belly in one efficient move and pulled the colt out of her womb, laying it in the grass beside its dead mother. He then pulled off his denim jacket and rubbed the colt briskly, wiping away the cheesy covering and blood. "C'mon, little boy," he said. "Breathe." He pushed and pulled on the little horse's ribcage. Finally, I saw the horse move.

I let out a whoop. "John, you're a miracle worker," I said,

John looked at me, smiling. "Behold, your brother, the horse." he said. "*Wakan Tanka niya waste pelo*," he said as he rubbed the colt's neck. *May God bless you.* Repulsed by the blood and sticky covering, I nevertheless stroked the little horse's flank and hugged him. "I'm really sorry about the mare," I said.

"Me, too," said John as he looked at the front of my bloody shirt. "You surprise me, Rainbow. I thought the messiness of life made you squeamish."

"Yeah. A little," I said. I stood and swatted the horsehair off my jeans, sending puffs of it into the air. "Death and birth is about as messy as it gets. Now you mention it, I could use a bucket of Clorox water."

"I can accommodate you there," he said, eyeing the colt. "I will call him 'Stranger' in honor of his sister who has not come to see her father in many moons. Let me think. Four years, River, since you've come to visit. We'll have a party! We'll call all the cousins! I'll contact the seven tribes!"

"Don't bother," I said, laughing. "Whenever you give a party, you end up giving away everything you own. The relatives come and stay a week and eat all your food and trash the place. Never mind all that. Just let's get my brother here settled in with a mare who'll nurse him."

"That shouldn't be hard," said John. "Many horses are roaming here since spring."

I had seen a few on my way in. When I was a kid on the Rez, horses were unrestrained. They'd walk down the street. Poke their heads in windows. Once I found a horse in John's living room when I left the door open. Now there was no longer free range and fences had sprouted up everywhere, but there were still a few breaks in those fences, and no one seemed in a big hurry to fix them.

"When you were little, you stuck to a horse like a flea on a dog's back," John said and smiled at the memory. "No saddle, no bridle. Just grabbed a hunk of mane and held on. I never knew any kid who could ride like you. You were a natural. Remember that?" I nodded.

"Toni," he yelled. I heard a door slam and she came running. When she saw us covered with blood, and the dead horse, she gave a low whistle. "Man, I'm so sorry," she said. "I know you loved that horse."

John dismissed her comment. "Look out in Jo Tinder's yard and see if that mare that lost her colt is still there. See if she'll let this little horse have dinner at her teats."

To me, he said, "Let's go to the house and wash up." Then, "Toni, find Uncle Charley and help him haul the carcass off with the block and tackle. It's bad medicine to have it on the land too long." With John, something was always good or bad medicine.

"C'mon, we'll go have some coffee," John said to me.

I followed him across the yard to enter by the back porch. Dried bunches of herbs hung from rafters, giving the place a dusty sage smell. In the kitchen, a few ants crawled on the amber bust of a Mrs. Butterworth syrup bottle left on the counter. A leather drum the size of a truck wheel and leather-wrapped drumsticks were propped in a corner.

John peeled off his shirt and sprayed it and his jacket with spot remover, then went into a bedroom off the kitchen and came back with a white T-shirt for me. I had him turn his back, and I took my bloody shirt off and slipped his on. He threw our shirts and his jacket in the corner by the drum.

Steam wafted from a tin pot of water atop a wood stove. He ladled some water out of the pot onto a rag, then wiped it through his short butch haircut and wiped his face. He wet another rag and handed it to me. Then he walked to the well on the back porch and lowered a bucket into it and pulled it up.

Water sloshed of the bucket onto the rough plank floor as he made his way to the sink, where he poured it in and added hot water from the tin pot. He motioned me over. We stood over the sink and scrubbed our hands and arms with a big yellow chunk of Lava soap.

"When are you going to move to the government housing?" I asked. "At least then you could poop without having to trck to the outhouse." Electricity had been run to John's house, but he had no indoor plumbing and still didn't seem in any hurry to get it.

"Highly overrated commodities," he said as he worked the soap into his sunburned knuckles. "I don't want any part of those boxes from Uncle Sugar." He rinsed and reached for a towel, then threw it to me. "I felt the pain flow into you from the horse," he said. "How long has that kind of thing been going on?"

I shook my head. "I'd like to pretend I don't know what you're talking about." The memory of the pain still throbbed behind my eyes. "But the minute I got off the plane I got a weird sensation. Some weird stuff has been going on with me. I sense things. And I sense that something seems off here with the animals."

"Maybe it's because you're back here. Near Paha Sapa. The sacred ground brings forth strange happenings. And, you're eighteen. That's when it began with me, too. The sacrifices of these Devil People, I believe that is stirring the animals up. I think that's the weirdness you're feeling. Have you heard of this?"

"Yes, but why would that be different? Animals die all the time," I said. "Meat packing plants...predators."

"That's true," said John. "But they're used to that—normal death. They understand the food chain concept. The Devil People scare them because of their intent. Every action of man is good or evil, depending on intent. Animals feel that evil."

"Colin's complained about losing some of his cattle to them. John, I don't want to feel animals' anxiety or know their thoughts. Is there some way to make this crazy thing stop?"

"Sure. Yeah," he said as he dried his hands. "Stop breathing.

That's the only way I know for sure. Why would you want it to stop? Why don't you accept this gift and use it to help animals and people."

"I don't trust it. It makes me feel crazy." I opened my eyes a little wider. "That's it. I've inherited schizophrenia from you. If other people found out, they'd know I was nuts. It's not normal, and I want to be normal. Besides, I'm only interested in helping two people right now. Mandy and her baby."

He seemed to take no offense at my comment and shrugged. "She's a puzzle, that one," he said. "After she got out of foster care I offered her a place here, but she wouldn't have it. So, a sister of her birth mother, Liz Two Toes, took her in. She and her Aunt Liz live in that old wreck up the hill." He motioned toward the window. In the distance, an old travel trailer and beat-up truck sat under a lone cottonwood tree. "Used to, she and Liz would go off somewhere for a few months, then end up back here. This time, though, she pulled in by me over a year ago." He placed a can of Pepsi in front of me. "The Pepsi's been hanging in the well so it's still cold. Sorry, no ice." He stirred some instant coffee and hot water into a cup for himself.

"Mandy never says much to me, but I catch her lurking around the barn sometimes, watching me. I knew she was pregnant. I could see it in her eyes before her belly got big. But she wouldn't talk of it. I've asked her what young buck got her that way." He took a sip of the hot coffee. "So I can put a can of whoop ass on him, you know? She doesn't know what I'm talking about." He shook his head. "What can I say?"

A small boy, about three, entered the kitchen and crawled onto John's lap. "This is Bruce. Belongs to Madeline Wilcox." He gave the boy's head a scratch. "Lost her man in Iraq. Terrible shame. She's in the living room there, with his baby." He shook his head. "He didn't even get to see the baby. She had nowhere to go, so I'm helping her out with a place to stay."

I can't say why that ticked me off. "It seems like you've turned into a regular Mother Teresa what with taking in Toni Thunderheart and Madeline's family," I said.

"It is the will of Great Spirit," he said, "for me to help where I can." He handed Bruce a kid-sized box of raisins and gave his butt a shove toward the door.

"Maybe you can do me a favor and talk Mandy into giving her baby up for adoption?" I said. "Aunt Angela and I, we can help her, if she'll come back to St. Mary's with us."

"She's afraid of me, Rainbow. She heard Uncle Charley and me kidding around once about how I put spells on people. She took it serious and doesn't want anything to do with me."

"I wish you could put spells on people," I said. Thinking of Billy, I said, "I've known a few people who could use a good curse."

"I'm not a trickster, Rainbow. I'm Pejuta Wacasa. A healer. If you want a curse, Uncle Charley is your man."

"*Our* Uncle Charley?" I asked.

"Yep," John said. "The best shamans deal with dark forces sometimes to help those who walk in the light. Of course, there are shamans who use the dark arts for their own purposes, but Charley is not such a one."

"How did Charley become a shaman?" I asked.

"He tells me this story. How years ago he was traveling through New Mexico. Bandits got him, buried him up to his neck. Occasionally they would pee near his head, laugh at him, or spit on him. They went away and he figured they left him to die. He was near crazy when the rain started. He prayed to Wakan Tanka. When the pooled rain came past his chin, he stopped praying and decided to let the Thunder Beings take him. Suddenly, lightning hit the ground. Charley says it split the ground clean in two, allowing him to crawl out. He couldn't hear a thing for six months and he was in pretty bad shape for a long time. He believes those bandits were actually other shamans, sent to rid him of his shadow self. He said he came out of there with the power to work with the shadow, for the betterment of others."

"If I only believed in that stuff, I'd ask Charley to put a spell on Mandy to let me take her to Kansas."

"Don't doubt that it's real. But I doubt Charley would do it. He's not big on messing in someone else's Walk. He probably won't see Mandy's situation like you do. He may think Mandy and those around her may need this lesson to grow. He will probably say things should proceed without his interference, since Mandy is not evil and no evil has been visited on her."

I slammed the cup down so hard my drink spilled out. "Dammit! Can't anybody help this poor kid out! Mandy can't raise this baby and I sure don't want Billy to do it! Can I petition the courts or something?"

"Do you really want to force Mandy to give up her baby? Do you think white man's court is going to care what happens to another Indian child? I'll help her as much as I can. Aunt Liz will help her, too. We Indians, we will take care of our own."

This from John who had left me to foster care. I knew how hopeless it could be for children on the Rez—drugs, alcohol and diabetes a constant in their lives. I wanted better for this baby.

John threw his coffee out the open window and set the cup down hard. "Billy Chance? Is that who it is?" He cracked his knuckles. When he spoke again, I could see he was making a conscious effort to unclench his jaw. "In this case, you can't control her or her baby's fate. Pray. Let Wakan Tanka take care of it." He hunched his shoulders. "Is 'bout all you can do."

"Let God handle it? Did you learn that in a twelve-step meeting?" I said, unkindly. He was clean and sober, but I still resented those wasted years.

"Yes," he said. "You'll find me at the meetings at Blessed Savior Church every Friday night. We start the AA meeting with the serenity prayer. 'God, give me the serenity to accept the things I cannot change, the courage to change the things I can, and the wisdom to know the difference.' That's a pretty good prayer."

"John, I have no serenity about this. I have courage, but I can't seem to get anything changed. And wisdom! All out. Zip. Nada. I have no idea where to get wisdom."

John said, "Don't worry. The opportunity to use your courage will come. Wisdom grows of making mistakes. You make a mistake. You get your butt kicked. You learn, and gain wisdom."

I smiled. "If I have no wisdom, I guess that means I've made no mistakes. Right?"

"Hey, there's plenty of time. You're young. I'm sure you will become very wise with a very sore ass. Speaking of a sore ass, how's it been with Colin? Has he forgiven you for being my daughter?"

"He's been nice," I said. "Even kind. It makes me wonder what he's up to."

"He's not so bad anymore," John said. "I've seen him around, talking to others in town. He's mellowed, probably because of Ruby. Like he was before your Aunt Bonnie died." He lowered his eyes. "I have to admit I am not blameless there."

"How's that?" I asked, taking a gulp of Pepsi.

"I never talked to anyone about this," he said. "It's painful, you know?" He trailed his finger through salt spilled on the table. "I've come to terms, though. When I was young and married to your mother, I was so full of myself. Ran with the young bloods, mostly causing trouble. Didn't want to work. But, you needed things, and I knew Briana was going to toss me out if I didn't change."

He looked away from me. "Bonnie was concerned for Briana and me and talked Colin into hiring me. I worked for him a few years and got to know Bonnie. I was able to hide my drinking pretty good then, you know, before Briana died. I worked cattle, mended fences, did odd jobs. Bonnie even had me babysitting for Blair. She trusted me completely. The summer that Bonnie was pregnant with their son, Colin put me to work painting their ranch house. Occasionally, Bonnie would bring out iced drinks. She and I would talk, mostly about the Indian Way. How we use herbs and peyote for childbirth. Do it natural. I told her how at the white man's hospital, even as late as the sixties, when the Indian girls gave birth there, doctors took the wombs, too." Little stress lines punctuated the corners of his mouth. "Young, healthy women. To cut down on Indian population. She was sweet, Bonnie was. These stories affected her. She decided not to go to a hospital. Have the baby at home.

"Colin argued with her about this, and he fired me. I figured that was the end of it, but on the day she went into labor she drove that pickup all the way out here. She was alone in my house when I found her in hard labor, the baby on its way."

He finally looked at me. "It went all wrong. She was bleeding heavy. When the baby came, he was stillborn, and her uterus came out with the baby. I did what I could. I got her to the hospital, but she had lost too much blood. Colin felt I killed his son and wife because I had talked her into staying away from the hospital. I swear I had not meant our conversations to affect her that way. Colin ran his truck clean through our house that night. Remember? I'm surprised he didn't kill all of us with that trick. Anyway, that's why he's always been hard on you, because you remind him of me. I'm surprised he has you in his house."

I put my hand on his shoulder. "That explains a lot," I said, and kissed his cheek. I pushed my chair back and stood. I felt weary. I was sorry John's mare had died. I was sorry he had worn this guilt all these years. I was sorry Colin had lost his son so many years ago.

Toni came in carrying Bruce and I noticed John stiffen in his chair. "We got the horse out, John," Toni said. "Grandpa's out in the pasture now on the backhoe, digging a hole for the carcass. Man, River, I'm sorry you had to go through that today," she said.

I shrugged and stood up. "I have to get back," I said. "Blair will be sending the cops out to find her car." I put my cup on the sink. I could feel my shoulders sagging. I was tired from seeking solutions and finding none. I must have looked it.

"Wait," John said. "Stay the night. It's been so long since I've seen you. Use Toni's cell phone and tell Blair you'll get her car to her tomorrow. There's a tower nearby. You should get a signal."

Toni handed me her cell, while Bruce ran to the other room. Blair didn't seem to have any problems with my keeping the car. She said she and Mandy had gotten into a fight and Ruby had sent Mandy home. She'd had to do the cleanup at the pool by herself. She was exhausted and was going to bed early and didn't have the energy to use the car anyway.

"I know what we need." John took my hand and led me outside to where three horses were munching hay out of the center of an old tractor tire.

"Whoa now," he spoke softly to them as we approached. He whispered in each one's hairy ear, then turned to me. "Okay," he said. He gave me a leg up onto the back of a big ginger horse, slightly squeezing the small of my back when he got me settled. Then he hoisted himself onto the other, a pinto. Toni pulled herself onto a small roan. I held tight to the ginger's mane, and nudged my knees into the horse's sides to give her a little gas. She took off like a cat with turpentine on her butt. We galloped across the plains, holding tight, John's horse keeping stride at my side. I glanced over to see him throw back his head and laugh, his sun-damaged face crinkling into fine lines like cracking glass. The horse's hooves churned up the smell of sweet grass and dust with every stride.

Toni's horse ran in front of me. Suddenly she threw both her hands up to the sky and whooped for joy, her legs clamped tight around the horse's barrel belly. She looked fine, and a little bit crazy.

The wind blew my hair back and I laughed for the first time in a long time, running across the rolling prairie. The horses finally spent themselves, and we turned back toward John's house. In the distance, Charley stood on the porch. I swear I saw my mother standing beside him, waving. Quickly, she turned to mist. I rubbed my eyes.

Did I hallucinate my mother? Did I see my mother's ghost? Or, is John right about Uncle Charley and he put a spell on me? If so, I couldn't think of a nicer thing he could have done.

Chapter Ten

Toni, John, Madeline and I spent a lot of the afternoon playing cards and talking. I went outside a few times to swing Bruce on the old tree swing when Madeline got up to tend the baby and Bruce got underfoot.

That evening, John lit up sage and fanned smoke throughout the house to ward off negative energies and I let out the remainder of the tightly held breath that I realized I'd been holding ever since I got off the plane. Then he rolled that huge drum out of the corner of the living room and beat on it and chanted. Madeline handed me an empty plastic Folgers container to drum on, and Bruce got an empty oatmeal box. I don't know what magic there is in beating on a drum (or in my case, an old coffee empty), but it made me feel marvelous. Toni surprised me by bringing out a flute. She blew music that was sad and haunting in some tunes, then lilting and joyful in others. Bruce danced through the whole thing, smiling for the first time since I met him. The baby seemed undisturbed by the noise, suckling at Madeline's breast and dozing.

After a while, Toni left us in the living room and headed to the kitchen. I followed and found her getting ingredients together to cook up some fry bread. I found a can of Spam, cubed it and fried it with onions. We piled the Spam and chunks of commodity cheese on the fry bread and called everyone in to feast. Madeline, Toni and I split the last can of Pepsi three ways. John stayed with his instant coffee.

Madeline's baby woke up, her cries calling Madeline out of the kitchen and into the bedroom. John followed her to help get Bruce to bed. After the crying continued through the cleanup and put away process, Toni and I looked at each other, nodded in silent assent, and headed outside for a walk and the night's silence.

Romantic lighting was provided compliments of Mr. Moon. Cicadas and frogs serenaded us as we kicked dirt clods with the toes of our tennis shoes. Moist night air kissed our faces and flowed around our bodies.

"What was it like, growing up here?" Toni asked.

I glanced over to see Toni's silhouette in the moonlight. "I didn't really grow up here. Mom and my sister and I left when I was five and moved into Pell Mell. But, I do remember good things. Some bad."

"Tell me one of the good things."

I tripped on a dirt clod and Toni gave me her hand to steady me. We continued to walk, hand in hand. "I remember Mom tucking me in at night. I remember prayer catchers John made hanging on my old iron bed frame. I remember John kissing her. I remember riding the horses."

"Tell me a bad thing."

I smiled. "I don't remember many bad times. Unlike many of the people on the Rez, we always had enough food. Mom made sure we were loved. Hmmm...Oh, yeah. Once, John brought home a young eagle. His friend, a Hopi holy man from Arizona, and he were going to take it down to Arizona with them and use it in a ceremony to bring rain." I took my hand away from Toni, reached down and pitched a rock I found. "This is a Hopi ceremony that does not end well for the eagle. They had planned to leave the following day, and John had tethered the eagle's leg to a log outside my window. I heard its pitiful squawk all night. Toward morning, I'd had enough and I couldn't stand the thought of that little eagle dying, so I sneaked outside and cut him loose. That was the one and only time I remember John spanking me."

"Harsh," she said. "I don't blame you for doing that. I love animals, too. Does he still use animals in ritual?"

"Haven't a clue. I know he respects it as part of some Native tribe's religious practices. I seldom got to see him after I left the Rez. Just the last couple years we've started writing letters, getting to know each other again."

"What else?" she asked. "I like the sound of your voice. Just keep talking."

"Let's see. I've learned not to get him started on certain subjects. Not now, but in the old days, it could trigger a bender that would last for days. Stuff like the things that happened here in the Seventies. Murders of AIM members. Fights between AIM and the FBI, the National Guard moving in. I've learned to steer clear of those topics around John. It was a war zone here for awhile and John was part of it. I don't know what part, but he's still friends with some of those activist guys from the old days. Still has bad feelings toward the government, and I can't say I blame him."

"Awesome," she said. "A real rebel. Do you think he's ...actively subversive?" she asked.

"No. It was a long time ago. It's just hard for him to let go of the resentment. What about you? Any good stories?"

"Naw." She swatted a mosquito. "Grew up following my dad around to base after base. Never lit anywhere long enough to make really good friends. I missed that." She smiled. "But I was in Arizona long enough to join the seventh-grade softball team. I got a trophy for my pitching. Led the team to victory. You should have heard the crowd roar." She laughed and thrust her hand out, snatching a mosquito in mid-flight.

I laughed with her as we had reached the barn. "Want to see some of my stuff?" she asked.

I wasn't sure what stuff she meant, but I was game. She slid the barn door back and I heard horse snorts and hoof shuffling and a few whinnies by way of hello from Stranger and his adoptive mother. We passed some stalls and Toni stopped, tugged on a chain and light flooded the space from a solitary bulb. We were in an area that used to be a tack room, four walls and a door with no roof and open to the hay loft above us. There were no longer saddles hanging in the room. John had probably sold or traded them long ago for booze when he was drinking, but the room still smelled of leather. A few bridles hung on posts, and a bucket of curry brushes and fly spray were in one corner.

Toni had swept away the dirt and straw and arranged a worktable where she could paint. It appeared she'd painted pictures on anything she could find—old barn wood, milk cans, pieces of old cars, old rusted saws. One unfinished project, a carving from an old stump, stood propped against the wall at the end of the worktable. "John discovered what I was doing in this room and had a fit," she said. "He was worried about having paint thinner and rags and paint in here. I saw his point once he mentioned it. I'd hate to be responsible for burning down his barn. So I put that stuff in a shed out back and now just have the paintings in here. Like them?"

"Yes. Especially this one of the wolf," I said, pointing to a piece of barn wood.

"I like that one, too. You can have it, by way of payment," she said. When I gave her a questioning look, she went on. "I really, really need a ride to town. There's a tourist trap on the highway there. They'll take my pieces, but I can't hitch in with all these. John won't let anyone else drive his old Cadillac and Uncle Charley has an old truck but never keeps gas in it. Until I sell the pieces, I can't afford the gas, either. Whad'ya say?"

"Of course," I said. "You don't need to give me anything for that."

"I'd have given it to you even if you said no. Because," she said, looping her arms around my waist, "I like you, River." Then, she did something I hadn't expected. She folded me into herself, kissing me. I wanted to push her back. I didn't want to seem easy. But, I darn near had an orgasm on the spot. She separated from me, her breathing ragged, and reached up, pulling the chain and plunging us back into darkness. The only light was that of the moon filtering through the wide open hayloft door above us.

"Can I do this?" she asked as she pulled up my T-shirt and slid her hands over my breasts.

"Yes," I said. I was human, after all.

"Have you ever been with anyone?" she asked as she kissed my neck.

This was my first time.

Frankly, no one had ever offered, except for lurid suggestions from my obsessed foster brothers. I knew I wasn't ugly. I think my world just hadn't been big enough to include sexual partners until now. Heck, I'd never even ridden on an escalator before. But, I sensed she was asking because she didn't want to be the first one, like maybe she might screw me up sexually forever.

"Sure, plenty of times," I said.

She pulled my shirt over my head and fingered my nipple, then latched her mouth around it and sucked. I went right up on my tippy-toes.

"Sweet Jesus," she said. "These things are like melons. We need to lay down." Next thing I know, we'd scurried up the ladder to the loft above us and were rolling each other around in the hay, literally. I didn't mind that I was such a cliché.

Shirts off, jeans unbuttoned, we were going for the gold in the French kissing competition. Then, she ran her hand down into my pants and found my crotch. I pulled away. "Don't put your fingers, you know, in there," I said.

She rolled off me onto her side and propped her head on one hand. "That's not how you roll?"

"I don't think so," I said. "It doesn't feel right to have your fingers in there...yet."

"Anything you want, River. Let's see if this is how you roll." She pulled me on top of her and rolled me completely over until she was on top again. Then she kissed little kisses all the way down to my jeans fly and unzipped me and tugged my jeans and panties farther down. Her tongue found that slim little piece of pink flesh wherein all fireworks are stored, and I discovered that this was definitely one of the ways I rolled. I came so hard I thought I broke my backbone.

"Done this plenty of times, huh?" she asked. "That was some kind of speed record."

I blushed. "Well, Ms. Lothario, maybe you can show me how it's supposed to be." With that, I lowered my head between her legs and pleasured her with my tongue as she had me. Watching her come was a sweet moment. It felt powerful and life-affirming to do that for another person. "Speed record for you, too," I said as we lay exhausted beside each other. We both laughed and embraced each other, igniting our bodies again. Loving again.

Next morning I hopped out of bed with pep in my step. I hoped that Toni had pep, too. I pulled on my jeans and T-shirt and walked to the kitchen. Evidently John was up, because the wood stove was hot and there was water on for coffee, but I didn't see him. I made some biscuits and put them in the wood stove oven. I pulled a cast iron skillet from the cupboard and put some flour, Hershey chocolate and sugar into it, and added a little milk. Then I put it on the stove and swished the mixture around, slowly adding more milk until I had a hot chocolate pudding substance. Bruce walked in, rubbing his eyes, and I plopped him down at the table and broke one of the warm biscuits open and covered it with what we at the shelter called chocolate gravy. As I was ladling some onto my own plate, I heard a door slam, and shouting.

"We made a deal. Don't even think you can back out," Toni was saying.

"That deal did not include my daughter," I heard John say. Then, I heard one of them shush the other as they approached the back door.

"What?" I asked.

"River, you're taking this witch into town, I hear," said John. "Well, don't let the door hit you both in the ass on your way out. I want her out of here pronto. Maybe when a couple days have passed I'll be able to stand the sight of her."

Well, this was unexpected. I couldn't imagine what he had caught in his craw today, but I had seen this schizoid side of him before, so it wasn't a shock. "Let me get my shoes and socks and keys," I said.

Toni loaded her art pieces into the trunk and backseat of

Blair's car, taking care to cover the seats with a blanket. Before I slid into the car, I turned one last time to look at John. His face was granite, but he motioned me over. "Watch out for that witch, Rainbow," he said. "She's not one of us."

"She's Charley's granddaughter," I said.

"He, more than anyone, knows who she is," he said, sadly shaking his head. He walked me back to the car and when I had settled myself into the front seat, he leaned in and kissed the top of my head, ignoring Toni. "Goodbye, Rainbow."

"Goodbye John." I couldn't help feeling I had disappointed him somehow, but I couldn't think how. I knew if he'd known Toni and I were together, he wasn't prudish enough to care. The Lakota language doesn't even have a word for homosexual, and their traditions include winkte, people of homosexual persuasion that are embraced by the tribe as those with special powers.

Inwardly, I puzzled on it all the way into Pell Mell. Toni wouldn't talk about their disagreement so I gave up and we turned to other conversation, enjoying each other, chatting about inconsequential things, and about our lovemaking, both of us getting turned on again. We stopped at Big Chief Trading Post out on the highway to unload her art, and then went on into Pell Mell to the YWCA where Toni assured me she'd be okay to stay. I tried to talk her into coming back to the ranch. I was sure I could talk Ruby into putting her someplace. But Toni wouldn't have it. We kissed each other long and sweet in the parking lot and I watched her go into the Y. "Neat girl," I said out loud to myself and smiled, then frowned as I remembered John had called her a witch.

Chapter Eleven

"What did you do to my car?" Blair circled the Mustang, hands on her hips.

I looked at the car. It looked the same to me. "Nothing," I said. "I put gas in it," I offered, in an attempt to soften up the tiny lines appearing around her mouth.

"How is it you can see filth in a kitchen, but you can't see it on a car? Look at this," she said as she drew her finger across the hood and presented it for my inspection. "Where the heck did you take it, the Australian Outback?"

"Just the Rez, like you said." I shrugged and added, "You know my dad lives off the beaten path."

"Your dad lives in the Twilight Zone," she said. "Did you two figure anything out? About Mandy, I mean? Did he do one of his spells? Throw some bones in a fire, spit on a four leaf clover? Something? Anything?"

"Nothing quite like that," I said, crossing my arms. "You can be sarcastic all you want, but I get the feeling you're more into the occult than you'd care to admit."

"Hey, I'm desperate. I'd try anything to get Mandy out of my life." She threw up her hands. "Who am I kidding. It's hopeless. She's hopeless." She turned toward the hood and wrote WASH ME on the hood, and leveled her eyes at me. "There's a new car wash on Porter Road. You can stop there after you take Mandy to Grandpa McKee's."

"Just hold on." I put my hand up like a traffic cop. "I'm not going anywhere near Angus McKee. I've never been invited to his house and I don't imagine he wants to hear from me now. So, no thanks."

"'Fraid you are. Mandy has been summoned," Blair said. "Ruby wants her out at Grandpa's to clean. She says Grandpa is raising the roof at all the 'dirtiness.' And, I'm not taking her. You got out of helping with the party cleanup. This is the least you can do."

No matter that Mandy was so pregnant she could hardly walk. I could see that Blair meant to make her have this baby on her lunch break, then get back to work. But Blair did look tired, and she had let me use her great car. "Okay, but only a drop and run." Then I had a thought. "How is it Angus lets Mandy in his house? She's as much Indian as I am."

"He doesn't know that. His eyesight isn't so good anymore. Ruby introduced her to Angus as her Italian cousin. He has no idea she's John's daughter."

"Ruby lied? How interesting."

"Well, yeah. I thought it was weird, too, her being so churchy and all. But she really needed Mandy's help with Grandpa. I don't think that's so bad. Do you? I mean, to lie if it doesn't hurt anyone?"

"Yeah, I do," I said. "I've learned when it comes to people to lower my expectations. I'm never disappointed."

Blair offered a crooked smile and crossed her arms. "It must be exhausting balancing on that pedestal all the time, St. River. Could be some day you'll fall off and join the rest of us mortals."

"No doubt. If I do I'm sure you'll be there to pull me further into the muck and mire."

Mandy came out of the house carrying a plastic laundry basket filled with bottles of cleaning supplies and rags and brushes. She moved slowly and dark circles smudged her eye sockets. I almost offered to help her clean Angus's house. I thought better of it. Angus hadn't wanted to see me before. He didn't now. I popped the trunk and Mandy dropped the supplies in, none too carefully. I saw Blair wince.

"You get Clorox in my trunk and I'll have your ass, bitch," Blair shouted.

Mandy smiled at me and got in, adjusting the seat to accommodate her bulk. I pushed in a Madonna CD, and carefully eased out of the drive so as not to spew gravel on Blair. Mandy turned around and flipped Blair the bird. I waved. We were off.

Visible from most anywhere in Pell Mell, Angus McKee's mansion stands like a sentinel on top of a bare knobby hill, surrounded by a black pointy wrought iron fence straight out of a Tim Burton movie. I sat outside the gate with Mandy, letting the car idle while I surveyed the place. Years ago the lawn had been lush and green. Now it was as yellow as an old man's fingernails. Four tall ionic columns supported a second-story balcony. Under the balcony, a door painted dull black boasted a huge gold lion head knocker. Potted trees that I remembered as trim and green now stood lifeless at either side of the door. No welcome mat in sight. It didn't appear Colin was breaking his neck seeing to the welfare of Angus's property. *Well, reap what you sow, old man.*

Mandy got out of the car and waddled up to input a security code onto a keypad. The gate swung open and she got back in the car. "Should I drive around back?" I asked Mandy. She looked back at me from weary eyes. She was taking a beating from her unwieldy bulk.

"No, I'm too fat. It's a long walk from the drive to the back door. I want the front door," she said. "I'll go in the front door like somebody special."

"Sure," I said. "No skin off my nose." I hadn't been planning to go in anyway. I pressed the pedal and we glided down the circular drive in front of Angus McKee's mansion and came to a stop.

"I don't want to go in. I hate that nasty man," Mandy said. "He makes me do stupid things, like wash the stupid cat. Then he'll say the cat doesn't smell right and make me do it again. Everybody knows cats clean themselves." She gave me a sly look. "Maybe if I make him mad, he won't want me to come back."

"Sure. Works for everybody else I know," I said, thinking of how he treated my mother and Aunt Angela. I came around and opened the car door for her. "Just don't do anything mean, like hurt the cat."

"I would never hurt an animal," she said, as she pulled herself out of the car.

I popped the trunk. I got out and followed her. She had wrapped her arms around the box of cleaning supplies, but the baby inside her was doing some weird anaconda movement and she was having a tough time getting hold of the box. "Let me help you carry that stuff into the house," I said, despite my desire to be off. She transferred the box to me and smoothed out her smock. "Be quiet, baby," she said. "Old Grouchy Pants might spank us."

The front door was unlocked and Mandy walked in. Images of large Russian wolfhounds stared down at me from tapestries depicting various hunting scenes hanging on either side of the front door. Large animal heads hung here and there. "Looks like the same decorator who did the Bass Pro shops," I said.

"I've always wondered where the back ends of those animals hang," said Mandy.

I wondered how it was for my mother to have been raised in such a place. I looked around. To my left opened a living room with little fruity French chairs no doubt due to Grandma Birdie's influence. A couple rooms with closed doors were on my right. A huge staircase with a dark wood banister rose directly in front of us. The banister looked good for sliding. Maybe Mom had enjoyed that, at least. An exquisite crystal vase, filled with dust-covered silk flowers, sat on a mahogany pedestal table in the middle of the foyer. I reached out to touch it and it nearly upended.

"Be careful of Grouchy Pants's stuff," said Mandy. "He hits when he gets mad. I'll be using most of that cleaning stuff upstairs. If you'll carry it up for me, I'll give you a big kiss. I'll take this 'fectant and get started in the kitchen down here."

Mandy went off to the kitchen and I stepped onto the first stairstep when suddenly I heard what sounded like soft humming from the room to my right. I stepped back and put the basket of supplies down on a French provincial chair by the front door. "Ruby?" I queried. I heard a growl. An overweight graying beagle sat under the chair, eying my ankle.

Ruby opened the door and stepped into the foyer, looking efficient in her white nurse uniform. "Don't worry about Soupy," she said in a whisper. "He's got no teeth." The old dog looked at me through malevolent yellow eyes. A badass Crip protecting his turf. I sensed I wasn't in danger of a bite from the old thing. I hadn't counted on a body block. He lunged, crashing into my legs, causing me to trip and knock the chair over. I grabbed for the tapestry to right myself and accidentally pulled the corner away from the wall.

"Oh, shit," I said, and felt myself turn red.

"Don't worry about that.". "It's ugly, anyway. Big old dogs snarling at a poor fox. Soupy, git!" she said and pointed her finger toward the back of the house. The old dog slunk away, crossing paths with Mandy who had come back to see what the commotion was.

"You're sure about the tapestry?" I asked. "I can tack it back up. If you need the gold leaf on that chair touched up, I know someone who's a good painter," I said, thinking of Toni.

"No, don't bother yourself a minute about it, hon. I'll see to it later," said Ruby, and she turned to Mandy. "Land's sake, Mandy, you might bust if you don't have that baby soon." When she saw Mandy's alarmed face, she said, "Oh no, honey, I don't mean that you really will bust." Mandy relaxed and blew a raspberry at her.

"I'm glad you're here, River. I let the temp go for a couple hours. Poor thing needed a well-deserved break. Himself," she continued, motioning with her eyes toward the room she had come from, "is taking his afternoon nap. Can you sit with him for a few minutes while I get Mandy started in the kitchen? I don't think he'll wake up, but if he does, all hell breaks loose if he doesn't think anyone else is in the house. Poor old thing has panic attacks all the time. I've just got to show Mandy how I want her to clean those kitchen cabinets so I'm going to be on a ladder for a bit. I don't think I'll be fast enough to get back here if I hear his bell. I need you to listen for him."

Off she hurried with Mandy, leaving me in the vestibule alone with the hounds of hell staring at me. Sighing, I picked up the various cleaners I had scattered and put them back in the box. *Please don't let him wake up*, I prayed. Tentatively, I opened the bedroom door and stuck my head in. I just wanted to see what he looked like. Angus lay sleeping peacefully. Thin skin stretched across tiny blue veins on his cheekbones. Small brown spots littered his arms and hands. His small chest rose and fell.

"Rock-a-bye-baby in the treetop," I hummed softly as I tiptoed into the room. A whistling noise came from his nose as he rolled over. I froze in mid-tiptoe, then relaxed a little and settled into a rocking chair when he gave a soft snore. A picture of Grandma Birdie and Angus sat on a doily on the dresser. People I came from but never knew. A smiling Colin looked back at them from another frame. No pictures of my mom or Aunt Angela. I folded my hands behind my head and propped my feet on a brocade footstool. As I leaned back, the rocker caught on a gold handled walking stick perched behind me, knocking it to the floor. The resulting crash must have had the Starship Enterprise putting up their protective force shields. Angus sputtered and sat up, rubbing his eyes. I scanned the room for a paper bag for him to breathe into for the panic attack I knew must be coming, but I seemed to be the only one in the room with panic.

"Ruby, damn you, you fat sausage," he yelled. "Can't an old man get some sleep?"

"Uh, she's not here," I said.

"Who are you?" he demanded.

"I'm River Morning Star, Briana's girl," thinking perhaps the years had softened him toward me.

He blinked and fumbled for his eyeglasses on the nightstand. "Briana! Ungrateful girl! I don't know her," he said. "And I don't know you. Get out! You're not welcome in this house."

He didn't have to say that twice. I flew out of the room as if leeches were on me. How could someone like that have raised my wonderful mother? I nearly bowled Ruby over as I made my way to the door.

"I'm leaving," I said. "I'll be back at two thirty. Please have Mandy out front waiting for me." I looked back at the skinny old apparition that was my grandfather through hot tears. Angus had already turned his back to me and was punching his pillow. "Certainly, River," she said. She circled her hand under my elbow as I headed out the front door. "Hon, your face is as red as a monkey's butt. Don't let anything that old poop says bother…" Suddenly, she was interrupted by a scream. We bolted toward the back of the house to the kitchen. Mandy was on her knees, holding her abdomen, covered with pickle juice from a broken jar. "Ooooh, it hurts," she said. "I fell off the ladder and my belly's hurting." I reached Mandy just as Angus appeared in the kitchen doorway.

"What the hell is going on here," he snarled.

"Mr. McKee! Get back in bed. I'll handle this," Ruby said. "See if Mandy can get up and keep her calm," she said to me. "I'll get some wet towels and dial nine-one-one." She rushed away.

I tried my best to soothe Mandy. From the sounds of Mandy's screams, she had a beaver in her belly trying to chew its way out. "Get out of my house," shouted Angus.

"Ruby's calling nine-one-one," I said. "The ambulance will be here in a minute. Believe me, I'll leave as soon as I can. Now shut up!" Angus blinked and stepped back.

"Make it go away!" Mandy screamed. "Get it out!" I had to remind myself that Mandy didn't grasp what was happening to her when pains like this came. She was obviously terrified. I guessed that the theory of hers about God putting the baby in the mother's tummy also assumed that it came out gift wrapped with no muss and fuss. She was scared and so was I. I took her hand.

"Sweetie, take slow deep breaths," I coached.

The paramedics arrived and bustled Mandy onto a stretcher. Mandy's contractions waned, but fat tears glistened on her cheeks. "There, there," Ruby patted Mandy's hand. "You'll be okay. We'll ride to the hospital and they'll check you out."

Ruby turned to Angus. "Get back in bed and get your rest, Mr. McKee. As soon as the temp nurse comes back, River will leave."

Resigned, Angus walked back into his bedroom.

To me, she said, "River, please stay until the temp comes back. She's due anytime now. Ardis is coming by to pick up some sheet music I want Little Elvis to sing at the wedding and I don't want Angus disturbed." Ruby grimaced. "It's my wedding, but she thinks she has to okay everything and Colin lets her get away with it." Then she was gone in a flurry of sounds and lights as the ambulance pulled away.

I wasn't crazy about staying. I wasn't crazy about seeing Ardis again and getting lectured about my sins. I looked at the sheet music. I knew this one. "What the World Needs Now Is Love, Sweet Love." All right, I thought. I'll stay because it's for Ruby.

I settled myself onto a couch in the living room. The old dog was back at his sentry position by the front door. "Too much excitement for me for one day," I said to the old dog. He left his post and circled me like a great white, his stiff legs goose-stepping around me.

"Get over yourself," I said. "You've got no beef with me."

He seemed to consider this, then jumped beside me onto the couch. A box of chocolates sat on the table beside us. I lifted the lid and an intoxicating smell wafted up. I took out a piece, which I shared with Soupy.

I gently pushed the old dog from the couch and got up to stretch. I yawned, my eyes resting on the downed tapestry, sadly hanging by one nail. I still felt bad about that. I'd hate for Mandy or Ruby to get blamed. I didn't worry about Angus abusing Ruby, but Mandy might get "hit" again.

Maybe I could fix it myself. I picked up the nail off the floor. I got a nutcracker off one of the living room tables, and balanced myself on the provincial chair. I spied the nail hole in the mortar and attempted to drive the nail back in with the nutcracker. When I swung at the nail, the chair under me wobbled, and I hit the brick in the middle instead of the nail head. The old brick popped in half and crumbs of mortar fell to the floor. The dog yelped in surprise and sniffed the offending mortar cautiously.

A satisfying four-letter word just fit for this occasion popped into my mind and nearly made it through my lips. It died in my throat when I spied a tiny piece of purple velvet peeking out from behind the broken brick. I pulled on it and the two pieces of brick came out in my hand, along with a velvet bag. I whistled softly as I opened the drawstrings and pulled out what I knew must be the Caitlen necklace.

Light from diamonds, rubies and emeralds danced in my hand. I'd never seen anything so valuable in my life. Their hypnotic hold on me lasted until I heard the rumbling of an approaching vehicle. A quick glance out a window told me I didn't want to be caught like this by Billy, who was pulling up in front of the house. I quickly shoved the necklace in my jeans pocket and crammed the two halves of brick together and wedged the nail in the mortar. Satisfied that the broken brick was hardly noticeable, I hooked the tapestry back over the nail, climbed down, and glanced out the window.

Billy was coming up the sidewalk. I sprang for the door and locked it. Through the door's peephole I could see him getting closer, whistling along to the country music blaring from his radio. He pounded on the door. I didn't answer. He squinted into the peephole.

"Mandy, let me in. I don't have all day." He continued to pound. Like a bad cold, he wasn't going away easily. I opened the door. Surprise in his eyes quickly slid away.

"Well, well, if it isn't Little Miss Ballbuster."

"You step toward me and I'll hurt you," I said.

"Oooooh, I'm scared," he said. "Just get a grip. I'm not here for you. This time. Ruby said she was leaving some sheet music. Mom told me to pick it up. Do you know anything about it?"

"Wait here," I said. When I returned, he was leaning against the wall with a cocky smile. I handed him the sheet music.

"So, how did the old fart handle your homecoming?" he asked. "Take you back all warm and fuzzy?"

"Not exactly," I said.

"Did you kick his ass like you did mine?" He laughed. "I

got to give it to you, River. Your wrestling skills have come up a notch."

He looked so totally at ease and sincere, I laughed, too. It was weird.

"Where is the old guy? He had some maintenance for me to do. Where's Mandy?" he asked, glancing around. "She told me she'd be here today."

"She's on her way to the hospital," I said.

"The baby?" Some emotion I couldn't place flashed in his eyes. Was it concern? When I nodded, he turned on his heel and ran to his pickup, got in, and laid rubber.

I sighed relief and shut the door. Unable to will myself to wait, I pulled the necklace out of my pocket and held it up to the light, its jewels reflecting light like a chandelier. Through their glow, I saw Angus peeking out of his room. Then things happened fast. "You thieving Indian," he yelled and rushed me, swinging that cane of his with more force than an old man ought to have.

He surprised me so, I dropped the necklace. I turned to run and he caught me by the ankle with that gold-headed stick and I hit the floor on my chin. Then, he clobbered me a few good ones across my back and to the back of my head.

"Jeez O' Peet, quit it you old fart!" I yelled, trying to scramble to my feet and covering my head with my arms.

"Old fart? Old fart? I'll knock the knickers off you, girl," he shouted.

He damn near did. I rushed out the door to the freedom of Blair's car, marveling at the agility of the old coot as he snatched up the necklace. I was just glad to escape and that he was too agoraphobic to chase me outside. I turned the key in the ignition, bolting out of the drive in time to pass the temp nurse coming from the other direction. Hoping, hoping, that she had a really large evil hypodermic to stick in that man's ass.

Chapter Twelve

I bought a bag of frozen peas at the Safeway and sat in the parking lot for awhile, holding it to my head, hating Angus. When I had devised several imaginary ways to kill him in terrible pain, I felt better. Ants and honey, a fiery pit, a pack of wolves, all good.

I got on the road again and went to the car wash to satisfy Blair. Then I stopped by the hospital. Ruby told me there was still no definite word on Mandy. Night came and found us still sitting in the waiting room watching a blur of blue-smocked personnel scurry about. I picked up a *Rolling Stone* magazine and marveled at how Keith Richards could still rock on.

Mandy had wanted Billy behind the green curtain in the emergency room with her and no one else. I'd occasionally see him go to the coffee machine or talk to a nurse or fetch ice. He looked glum and tired, which I imagine pretty much mirrored the look of Ruby and me. The nurse finally told us to go home since it could be hours before we knew one way or the other about what the baby was going to do.

I was anxious to get back to the Bonnie B to tell Aunt Angela about the necklace. What I found instead was her note taped to the fridge. "I've gone to Mt. Rushmore with the relatives. We may go on from there to Lead to do some gambling. Wish me luck! Be back late. Love, Ang." Having seen her cell phone plugged in on the kitchen counter, I knew there was no way to reach her. Disappointed, I watched TV with the cat in the living room, then went to bed.

Next morning I crawled out of bed around eleven, showered, and put on jeans and borrowed one of Blair's Anne Klein button-up shirts and walked downstairs. There was yet another note on the fridge from Aunt Angela, but the cell phone was gone. I tried to ring her, but she must have forgotten to turn it on. This time the note said she'd gone souvenir shopping.

"Crap," I said as I passed the cat on my way to the porch to wake up with the newspaper and a Pepsi. As she shamelessly rubbed around my ankles begging for cream, the phone on the porch rang. I pushed her aside and rushed to answer it. It was Ruby calling from Angus's house, reporting the events that occurred since she'd seen me.

The hospital had sent Mandy home. They'd been able to stop her labor, and she had a little soreness from the fall, but was otherwise okay. When Ruby got back to check on Angus, he had been ranting about being attacked by Indians and she gave him a sedative. And, the dog died.

Ruby had found Soupy dead beside an empty box of candy and shredded chocolate wrappers. Chocolate causes seizures in dogs and is often lethal, she told me. She said she thought that Soupy must've eaten the whole box, although the old dog had never before shown the slightest interest in the candy on the coffee table. She didn't understand what could have gotten into the old beast. Gulp. My stomach dropped into my toes. *There should be skull and crossbones on the box!*

A meaner person would have been glad. Karma in action, right? The old man beats me, so I accidentally off his dog. I felt truly awful, sorry for the pain that Angus must be feeling at the loss of his longtime friend. I couldn't imagine a feeling much more wretched than this—accidentally being responsible for ending the life of another living, breathing being.

"My bad," I admitted softly into the phone. "I fed the dog a piece when I was there. It must have enticed him to have more." Ruby was silent for a moment. Then she surprised me by laughing. "Oh, well, I guess death by chocolate isn't so bad," she said. "The poor thing was old and would have died soon anyway. You saved Angus the hard decision to have him put down. Don't worry a minute about it. I won't tell Angus it was you."

"Man, I feel so...I just..." A knock at the door kept me from getting maudlin. Through the glass I could see Pell Mell's finest at the door.

"That can't be good," said Ruby when I told her. "Buster is a friend of Colin's, but I just can't warm up to him. Watch your back." I knew there was a reason I liked Ruby. I hung up, and opened the door.

Buster tipped his hat to me, then slid it off his tanned chrome dome head, giving me the up and down. About six feet two, he resembled Billy. But where Billy was lanky, Buster was hard as a Green Bay Packer lineman under that uniform. "River. It's been a long time. I need a word," he said, pushing me aside to enter the porch. I stepped back, then noticed Ed and Tula staring out at the prairie from the Adirondack chairs and motioned to the couch inside the living room.

I quickly scanned the living room with a critical eye. It appeared that someone had run a dust rag over everything and put fresh flowers on the shiny pine wood coffee table. As I walked past the table, I picked up a few magazines and lined up the edges. I sat down, making sure my knees were together in the ladylike fashion Aunt Angela had taught me. I stacked the coasters, then felt totally irritated with myself that I cared a whit about what he thought. Buster came around the other end of the coffee table to join me on the couch. I could hear the swish of his starched pant legs as he moved past me.

"Nervous?" he asked as he removed his hat with manicured hands, nails buffed to a shine. Sharpshooter medals were stacked on top of his crisp tan shirt pocket like Tetris cubes.

"Of course not," I said. "Why would I be nervous?" Tsunami

waves of perspiration rolled off me. Last time I had seen Buster was when my mother had died. I had been a child yelling at him about what a liar he had for a son.

"Colin's around here somewhere," I said, hoping Buster would have some business with Colin. Perhaps this was about the mutilated cattle and not about my fiasco with Angus. I looked for an excuse to get out of the room. "Coffee while you wait?" I asked.

"No." He smoothed his hand over his shaved head, and leaned forward. "I'm here to see you." The too-sweet scent of his bay rum cologne violated the air between us.

Relax, I told myself. I spread my arms wide, placing one on the back of the couch, and leaned back, hoping by suggestion that he would relax as well. He continued to sit like he had a poised cobra for a spine. "I hope we're past grudges, you and I," he said. "But whether you harbor ill will for me or not, I feel honesty is the best policy. So. My wife tells me you still have a mouth on you. What I need are answers, not smart mouth bullshit."

I blinked. Talk to me like that. Yeah, that's the way to bring out the Miss Congeniality in me.

"I understand you were out at Angus's place yesterday," he said. "He reported a necklace missing this morning. A crucifix, worth about three hundred thou, he says." He leveled his eyes at me. His eyebrows, perfect crescent moons, twitched. I wondered if he tweezed them.

"He says you actually had the necklace in your hand. He says you dropped it, but he thinks you came back later and took it. Now's the time to come clean about anything you saw, heard or did while you were there. Anything."

I blinked. A white-hot shiver ran up my spine. Anger mostly, but a little fear threaded through. "Angus is hallucinating. The only thing I saw while I was there was a hard time from Angus and your son," I said. The memory of how those jewels sparkled in my hand was still fresh, but I would go to hell for lying before I would admit anything to this jerk.

"My son?"

"Yes. He came by, he said, to pick up Mandy."

He stared at me and said nothing for so long that I thought perhaps he hadn't heard me. His left brow arched so high I thought it would snap like a rubber band when he finally said, "I knew it would be hard to curb that smart mouth bullshit for long. But to keep the peace, I'll pretend I didn't hear that accusatory tone in your remark. Billy did not take that necklace."

"I didn't say that," I said. "I just said he was there. But I can't pretend I didn't hear your tone. You think I took it."

"Well, if the moccasin fits…" he said, and smiled.

I gave him a Lisa Presley stare. "You think that's funny?"

His smile slid away. "All right, River, this is how it shapes up. Your being in Pell Mell isn't good for Billy. That ruckus you made about him killing your mother years ago traumatized him so bad we had to take him to a shrink. To top it off, when you couldn't convince the judge with that lie, you then came up with that stupid business the day before of Billy's supposed assault on you in the school basement. You couldn't pin a murder on him, but he got six months in juvie for that supposed attack. He was a mess for a good couple years and seeing you just brings all that back."

"I didn't lie about anything. When Mom died, the policeman asked me straight out what possible motive I thought Billy would have had for wanting to kill my mother. I just answered his question with the only explanation I could think of. He'd killed her to get even with me because I got him in trouble when I ran screaming to you during your conference with Mom. And, he'd had his wangie hanging out. Remember? I was standing next to Billy when you hit him so hard it nearly knocked *my* teeth out."

"You were such a stupid little girl with a big imagination," Buster said. "I want you to give up this vendetta you have against Billy."

"What vendetta?"

"Don't tell me it wasn't your idea to entrap my son by getting that retarded sister of yours to seduce him and get pregnant." He smiled like a hyena. I had never before noticed that Buster's canine teeth protruded slightly. "What a clever way to make him pay for the rest of his life, plus take care of Mandy for the rest of hers," he said.

"I never..."

"Save it," Buster said.

I was desperate to slap Buster. I nodded. "Okay." This guy was so cracked. I just wanted him out of the house.

"How long will you be in Pell Mell?" he asked.

"I plan to leave after the wedding."

"You and I wish. I need you to stay around a little longer," he said. "Angus thinks you stole the necklace." His brows stopped twitching as his eyes bore into mine. "I think you did, too. But I can make the charge go away, if that's the price I have to pay to have you and your retarded sister leave Billy alone."

"I didn't take it!" I insisted.

"I want you to think hard about calling Mandy off. Otherwise, things could get, well, complicated." He turned to go, calling back, "You know, you look a lot like your mother. Try to be smarter than her. Don't get too close to the edge."

Chapter Thirteen

Weariness hung on me like a wet sweater. I sat on the couch not knowing what move to make next. I desperately wanted to leave Pell Mell. It was obvious that nothing I could say would change Mandy's mind. I let my head slump forward into my hands. What could I possibly do to convince Buster that I hadn't stolen the necklace?

I went to the bathroom and rubbed some Vicks VapoRub on my nose to get rid of Buster's cologne smell, then headed for the kitchen to get some water. Out the window I saw Ruby's assorted relatives in the pool, playing Marco Polo. White thighs bumped and cellulite rippled as they floated on donut-shaped pool toys. If they were back, maybe Aunt Angela was too, but I didn't see her by the pool. I'd go looking for her later because frankly, I didn't feel so hot. I felt all shivery and cold. I realized I was losing control. Busting into a big fat cry felt imminent.

I set my drink on the counter and took a deep breath. I picked up a rag and wiped something black and ugly off the stove. I looked around. Small puddles indicated people had tramped to the bathroom from the pool. A few empty Coke and beer cans were on the counters, dirty dishes in the sink. Wet towels had been shoved behind the door and something that looked like brain matter had exploded in the microwave.

I needed to clean. It would bring my sanity back. A mantra marched through my mind. "Busy hands are happy hands." Mother and I used to sing that together as we cleaned house. I opened the broom closet, got out supplies and got busy. After two hours of steady scrubbing appliances and floors, and cleaning out the fridge and some cabinets, I felt better.

Good and tired, I could relax by the pool. I headed up to Blair's room, pushed myself into my oh-so-not-a-thong two-piece swimsuit I got at the outlet mall and headed out. On my way I knocked on Ruby's bedroom door to see if Aunt Angela was there. No answer. Maybe she was napping. Oh well, the good news/bad news had waited this long, it could wait awhile longer.

It appeared most of the relatives had gone back to the motel. The few that remained in the pool waved and smiled, but I wasn't feeling chatty. I managed a meek smile as I fell into a chaise and lay back. Buster had scared me, but I had made myself too tired to worry about it now.

I closed my eyes and pictured Toni's face, wondering what she was doing, when I'd see her again. I mused over our night together in the barn. Sunlight baked my bones and laughter and conversation in and around the pool soothed me. Splashing water muted into a pleasant backdrop for a beautiful dream. My mother was sitting by the pool with me. She walked to a tree and pulled out a bird's nest with a tiny bluebird in it. "You must take care of the small bird, River," she said. She smiled, and was handing the bird to me as I awoke.

The sun was going down. Everyone was gone. Someone had put a large beach towel over me and pulled an umbrella table over to shade me. On the table beside me was another note. "Gone out with Ruby and Colin. Be home late. Ang."

Poop. Was she deliberately trying to avoid me?

I pulled myself up and headed to the kitchen. I picked up

the phone and dialed Aunt Angela's cell, leaving a message that I must talk with her. The scent from something barbecued drifted on the air, but I ignored it and helped myself to an orange and an apple from the fruit bowl. I could hear others talking and the clicking of balls coming from the recreation room down the stairwell off the kitchen.

I didn't want company. I was depressed. I wanted to dream of my mother again. I went to Blair's room and lay down on the bed, still in my swimsuit. I covered myself with a light comforter and tried to get back into the dream, but the only thoughts coming to me were of the crap that had happened since I stepped off the plane.

I heard what sounded like gunshots. I looked out the window and knew immediately what I was hearing. Billy hadn't been out to work with Darkwater and the horse had probably spent all day in the barn. The stallion was making a ruckus, kicking the stall walls and his tin water bucket. He was restless, or maybe there was a skunk in the barn. Or something more ominous, like a bobcat? I thought of John's pregnant mare.

I yawned. I wanted sleep, but my conscience niggled me. I couldn't let Darkwater hurt himself. I pulled some Levi's on over my bikini bottoms and slipped my feet into tennis shoes. I grabbed one of Blair's long button-up shirts off a hanger and put it on over my bikini top.

I didn't want to run into a two-legged so I crawled out the window and onto the porch roof. I shimmied down the tree and crossed the dirt lane to the barn. The smell of ozone mingled with dust and lavender from the herb garden. The wind blew a chill down my neck. In the darkening twilight, I padded through the open barn door and approached Darkwater.

"Whoa, boy," I murmured. He settled at the sight of me. I ran my hand down the blaze on his face. "What's the matter here?"

Ask a question. Get an answer. A smoky bubble formed over his head, but I turned away. I didn't need a hallucination to tell me what the matter was. His body language was clear enough. He was tired of being confined. I knew exactly how he felt. I stroked his neck, his shiny body under my hand rippling with pent-up energy. He pawed the ground.

"How 'bout I just take you out of this stall?" I said, wondering if that would be the last original idea I ever had. "Would you let me get on your back, baby?" I asked. "Would you, sweetie?" I cooed as I leaned against his side.

The massive stallion wasn't put off by baby talk. I sent him a picture of me on his back. He snorted, blowing hot air out his nostrils, and nudged me with his head. I took that for a yes. I didn't bother with a saddle or bridle. I slid the stall latch, and invited him to follow.

Once out of the barn and into the corral, I grabbed his mane, pulled myself up onto his back, and swung my leg over. He snorted and stomped in a version of the horsy cha-cha. I had in mind a nice little saunter, but when he snorted and put his head down, I knew I had better hold on. He reared up. When his forelegs hit the ground, he shifted into high gear on a dead run and cleared the fence. It occurred to me that maybe this idea should have been left swirling in the bowl.

Wow! He ran hard into the night. Trees sped by in a blur. With only the moon for light, Darkwater jumped ruts and ridges that I couldn't see. I prayed he wouldn't step in a hole and break a leg. In the distance, lightning silently streaked across the sky over the Black Hills. The wind was picking up.

How far had we come? How fast was that storm moving? We needed to find shelter. No telling how Darkwater would react to thunder. I didn't want to be on his back when I found out. Bailing off seemed suicidal, but saying "whoa" wasn't having an effect.

I fixed a mental picture of Darkwater stopping, and prayed. Finally, he slowed, his sides heaving. He trotted across a gully and started tracking down a dirt road. He came to an intersection and looked both ways as if checking traffic, then took a left, trotting to a stop next to a bulldozer by a clump of trees. Sporadic raindrops plopped on my face.

I slid off Darkwater's back, trying to catch my breath. A bulldozer loomed beside me like a giant lightning bolt magnet. I moved away from it, trying to see where we were. Darkness swallowed Darkwater, but slowly other shapes merged together and formed objects. I spied a pile of twisted and torn mud-covered tree roots the bulldozer must have uprooted. A lone stadium light shone in the distance, keeping watch over other heavy equipment, stacks of picnic tables and iron barbeque pits. A flatbed truck held creosote-drenched logs. I heard a fish jump and turned to see an expanse of black water behind me. This had to be Hannibal Lake, under construction.

Cabins in various stages of completion were barely visible. Most were just frames attached to concrete slabs. A couple had chimney construction started. One was complete. I headed to it, hoping it wasn't locked. I turned the knob. No luck. Shut up tight.

Thinking the place empty, I attempted to open a window when suddenly a light glowed inside the cabin. It appeared to be from an upstairs loft. Enough light shone on the downstairs that I could see the layout of the living room through the front window. Knotty pine paneling and shiny wood floors gave the cabin a homey rusticity. A range hood light shone dimly from a small kitchenette at one end. The only furnishings were a couch and chair covered in black-and-white cowhide and a couple end tables and a coat rack.

I saw what looked like a black cloak on the rack beside a denim jacket that looked like it might be the one Billy wore. A small book lay on the end table beside it. I could just make out the title, *The Luciferian Primer*, by Salmud Skeazy. I wasn't too familiar with the book, but I knew it contained rites for satanic worship. I had picked it up once while browsing through a used book store. It wasn't my kind of reading, but I was intrigued enough to Google Salmud Skeazy on my foster brother's computer.

Dead now, Skeazy had considered himself a high priest of the devil. As I recalled from my quick investigation, a large part of his belief was that you could get great materialistic rewards here on earth if you sought the favor of the Prince of Darkness. This was accomplished through various rites, orgies and the blood sacrifice of animals. A bunch of other links popped up with information about human sacrifice as well. Evidently, these wackos believed that blood had great power in calling forth the devil, especially the blood of the young. I thought about Colin losing his livestock to a cult, most of them baby calves.

Was this where Billy lived? I shivered in the cold and chewed on a fingernail thinking it might not be a good idea to confront Billy alone in the dark. I turned to tiptoe away.

Suddenly, I sensed movement in the living room and flattened my back against the cabin. Through the window, I saw Mandy. She switched on the kitchen light and pulled a Coke from the fridge. When she was nearly to the stairs to the loft, I saw her eyes light on the *The Luciferian Primer*. She picked it up and flipped it open. Then, she purposely strode toward the door, opened it, and pitched the book out in the yard. She must have barely missed seeing me dive to the dirt.

I didn't want Mandy to see me. She might inadvertently mention to Colin that I'd been out here. If Darkwater didn't make it back to the ranch, Colin might wonder how his horse got out and how I got out here and put two and two together. I was considering whether it might be easier just to 'fess up and go knock on the door and ask for Mandy's help when I spied the book laying in the dirt, partially hidden by the tire of an old scooter.

I checked the scooter for a key. Of course it wasn't there. If it weren't for sucky luck, I'd have no luck. I picked up the book and stuck it in the waistband of my jeans and walked away. If Billy was in there with Mandy, I was staying out here.

I walked away from the cabin, trying to get a fix on where Darkwater might be, then sat on a rock and finished picking stickers out of my pants legs as lightning sawed across the sky. Thunder accompanied it this time, banging and clanging against the sky like my thoughts about Billy being in a satanic cult.

Was this why he was so interested in Mandy? A bitter taste clung to the back of my throat. Had he graduated from sacrificing cows to humans and wanted Mandy's baby? Fearing for her now, I marched back to the cabin prepared to do battle with Billy if I needed to. It was dark inside and there was no answer to my pounding on the door. The scooter was gone.

Focus, I told myself, or be caught in the storm. I remembered a place we kids used to play, farther down the shoreline, where a ledge extended out of a sheer rock wall high above the water. At the top of that ledge was a natural spring that spilled its contents into Hannibal Lake. The resulting waterfall and foliage camouflaged a cave that would accommodate Darkwater and myself. The existence of the cave wasn't secret, but only the most adventurous of us kids wiggled past the Do Not Enter signs. Tonight I planned to go in only far enough. After all, there is no dark like the dark of a cave.

I continued to look for Darkwater on my way to the cave. I hoped he hadn't taken off at the sound of the thunder. My stomach clenched as I thought of any harm coming to him. Blair would kill me, and I wouldn't blame her. What a dork I had been to ride out here in the dark.

I finally saw him standing under a willow tree, its branches hanging over his back like skinny snakes. I approached him making soothing sounds, but he whinnied and shied away, obviously bothered by the thunder. The wind caused one of the branches to lash out, and Darkwater took off. I prayed he had the time and sense to make it back to the Bonnie B before the storm hit in full fury.

Sounds caught my attention. Chanting? I peeked through a thick wall of willow branches. About fifty yards away, a small campfire glowed. What looked like a kerosene camping lantern had been placed on a rock. Headlights from an old truck provided extra light. About ten people in hooded black robes surrounded the campfire. One of them was wearing snakeskin boots. That had to be Billy. I remembered those boots from when he was straddling me in Blair's room.

A young woman with flowing burgundy hair and white, almost translucent skin danced naked around the fire. My heart did a curious flutter. Who knew Blair McKee had a tattoo there?

Chapter Fourteen

What the heck had Blair gotten herself into? As if to get my erratic heart into rhythm, a lone drum began a steady beat. The fire threw shadows against Blair's skin as she wiggled and danced around the fire.

A tall figure robed in red seemed to be in charge. He lifted his hands and the drumming stopped. Blair gyrated a moment more until she realized she had lost her accompaniment. She turned to Red Robe and the firelight caught her expression. She was grinning, like when she used to finish one of her pom-pom squad routines, or had done a perfect cartwheel. Red Robe said, "Bring forth the sacrifice." One of the other robes walked to his car and pulled out a small, noisy goat.

The grin slid from Blair's face. "Nooooooo!" she yelled. Then, she made a grab for the goat. A goat tug of war commenced, just as the skies opened up.

"Ah, damn," I said to myself as I saw another hooded figure step forward, brandishing a large knife. Blair screamed, won the goat and ran away through the pouring rain. It appeared the goat had fainted, its body stiff in Blair's arms. The guy with the knife was not far behind.

I bolted out of the willows, yelling, "Stop, stop." Probably not the smartest thing I could have done, considering all eyes turned toward me. Yikes! I did, however, take some attention from Blair, who was still holding onto the goat, running in circles and trying to avoid the knife blade slashing at her back.

I spied Blair's Mustang. Despite the rain, Blair had the top down. Had she been drinking? Hadn't she noticed the approaching storm? I ran to it, hoping the key was in the ignition. I jumped in, turning the key in almost the same movement. The engine roared and I gunned it. I made a few runs around the grass, bumping into ruts and sliding on cow pies and mud. Black, hooded figures, rolled aside as I advanced on them. Once alongside, I yelled at Blair to jump in. Goat tucked under her arm like a football, she lunged head first into the backseat, just as I caught another robed figure on the hip, spinning him around onto my hood. I tried to push him off, but his robe was hung up on the car windshield. Imagine my surprise when I yanked his hood off and it wasn't a him, but a Toni. Totally pissed, I reached down and yanked her into the seat alongside me by her belt loops. The moron with the knife threw it, a close parting shot. Blair's white ass mooned her tormentors as we outdistanced them.

"What the hell?" said Blair turning to Toni. "Who are you?"

"I can explain," said Toni in a suspiciously calm voice. Except for probable bruising, it didn't appear either one of them was hurt.

"Explain? Explain! What was that?" I yelled at her, as we got back onto paved road. I brought up the convertible top and turned on the heater.

"That was the biggest mistake of my life, that's what that was," Blair said, thinking I was speaking to her and wiping rain off her face as she leaned over my shoulder from the backseat.

"You think? How'd you and Toni get yourself messed up in that?" I demanded.

"It was stupid, I realize that now," said Blair.. But to get rid of Mandy, I was willing to try anything. This guy I know, Hector, he said this cult stuff really works. He said he'd talk to the head of the coven so they could do a rite to make Mandy so uncomfortable she'd leave town. I figured if it didn't work, where's the harm? You know, just a bunch of kids getting together, barking at the moon and getting drunk and dancing around a fire naked. I had no idea that they were killing animals! They were going to kill Horatio!" She patted the head of the little goat. "How dare they?" The fainting goat I had seen penned by the barn awoke and nuzzled as far as it could into Blair's armpit. Blair's eyes widened as realization set in. "They almost killed me!"

"How could you not know they were killing things? Your father has been losing cattle all spring," I pointed out.

"When he talks, I zone," replied Blair. "Who is she?" she asked, turning toward Toni. "Do you two know each other?"

"I don't know. I'm waiting to see," I said.

Toni smirked and tried for a lame smile. "We seem to have lost them," she said. I slowed the car to forty. The downpour had stopped, replaced by a fine mist. "It's like with Blair," she said. "I was just curious. That's all. I'm not one of them."

"I hope they don't try to get even with me later," Blair said. "I don't know who they were, but they know me. They know where to find me. New York isn't sounding like such a bad idea is it, River?" I might have agreed, but with the stolen necklace rap hanging over my head I was sure if I left town I'd be the number one suspect, and Buster would haul my ass back. Yep, this little incident was typical Blair.

"You're such a freak, Blair," I said.

"I know," Blair said. "I was stupid." Toni just looked away.

"You, Blair I believe. I know you're an idiot," I said and slammed on the brakes, having made a decision. "Toni, even though I haven't known you long, I know you're smart. I doubt you could have gotten involved in something like that without fully knowing what it was. Get out."

"Ri...iv...er," she said. "Don't be this way."

"Get the fuck out!" I said, tears in my eyes. What was it she had said to me? She loved animals? Full of lies. Toni opened the door and stepped out. I looked back at her as I pulled away. She looked dejected and cold, standing there in the dark in that stupid cape. Man, could I pick 'em.

"At least, Darkwater is safe in the barn," Blair said. "I don't know what I'd do if those crackheads ever got hold of him."

I gulped. "Yeah," I said. "Me, too."

Chapter Fifteen

"What do you mean, he's not in the barn?" Blair shouted from the backseat as we bumped down the lonely country road. She was naked and dripping wet. Yet, freaky intimidating.

I hemmed. I hawed. I picked at a cuticle as I drove. Finally, I spilled about taking Darkwater out for a night ride. "I'm sure he's okay, though," I added.

"How can you be sure?" she snarled. "His autopilot hasn't been installed as far as I know."

"He's smart enough to find his way back."

In the rearview mirror, I saw her lips push out a pout so far I thought she might quack. "If anything happens to my horse, swear to God, physics will not explain how you got so pretzel-shaped," she said.

"Relax," I said. "The important thing is I saved your butt back there." I didn't think it would hurt to remind her of that. She had a mad on, that was for sure.

"If Darkwater doesn't get home, Daddy will freak. If I tell

him you lost my horse, I doubt he'll think you're the responsible person he wants to accompany me to New York. I'm tempted to tell him, though, just so he'll give you the butt kicking you deserve for being a dildo."

"I'm a dildo?" She had a nerve. "You won't tell him. If you do, I'll tell him how I found you dancing naked and barking at the moon, brainiac."

"He wouldn't believe you."

"No, but Aunt Angela will. She'll convince Ruby and you know Colin will do whatever Ruby wants."

She wasn't happy with me, and nearly choked on the words, but she said, "All right. If you say so. He'll find his way home." The little goat was bleating madly. Blair shouted, "Shut up," and it keeled over. "What a mess. I can't believe I left the top down."

"You shouldn't have been drinking." I sounded too good even to myself.

"I wasn't drinking. Stop the car," Blair suddenly shouted, "I need to drive. I just saw Raphael."

"Pardon me?"

"Raphael, my other goat. I just saw him. He's out there, all alone, in the dark." Blair tugged on my shoulder. "Those weirdos must've tried to take him, too. Thank God he got away. We need to trade places so I can go back for him. I need to drive."

"Nope. You've been drinking."

"I tell you, I'm sober. Oh, here." She extended her long naked legs between the bucket seats and tried to slide around the stick shift into the front passenger seat. For the next few seconds I saw moves I thought were anatomically impossible.

"Oh, all right!" I pulled over, put the 'Stang in park, and walked around to the passenger seat while she slid over into the driver's seat. As the motor hummed in idle, she handed me the goat, adjusted the seat, and sat there staring at me. "What?" I said.

"Hello? I'm sitting here naked. Aren't you going to at least offer me my blouse? I'm cold."

My eyes slid down to her boobs. Yep, she was cold. I shoved Horatio into the backseat, feeling grateful these guys came with little stubby handles on their heads. I took off the blouse and handed it to her.

Blair did a U-turn and took a left down a dirt road, slowing the car to look the area over carefully. "There's a flashlight in the glove compartment," she said. "Grab it and shine it over there. That's where I saw him."

We spied Raphael a few feet from the road munching grass in the moonlight. I was excited to see Darkwater grazing beside him. Blair pulled over, jumped out and headed for Raphael. Raphael trotted away, accompanied by Darkwater. Too mad to follow, I tossed her the flashlight and watched its beam bob as she moved. Its light kept going out and coming on again. "Damn cheap light," I heard her say. Then, "I've got him," she said, as the flashlight went out again.

Then she screamed.

I was out of the car and running toward the scream, tripping over a tree stump, barbed wire and a dried cow skull, I think. I found Blair on her knees bending over what looked like a lumpy pile of black laundry. The flashlight came on again and I saw one of the hooded cultists lying on the ground. The small scooter I'd seen earlier by the cabin was now a pile of crumpled steel nearby. I heard a soft moan. I couldn't tell if it came from me or Blair or the person on the ground. I rolled the figure over.

"Jesus, it's Mandy," I uttered.

Her eyes flickered. She moaned again. Blood was smeared across her cheeks from a gash on her forehead. I pulled back the black robe to look for other injuries. An upside down cross hung from a beaded cord across her chest. Her legs, sticky with blood, were going in the wrong direction. One leg was attached only by a little skin at the thigh. The bones of the other leg were sticking out of the skin. I felt her touch my hand, then pull it to her belly. "Car," she said.

Tears stung my eyes. "You'll be okay," I lied. "We'll call nine-one-one. Someone will come. Just hang on."

"No," she whispered. "I see Momma." I looked around, seeing nothing. "Save...my...baby," she pleaded in gasps.

My mind was a blur of moment-to-moment sensory input. The copper smell of blood. The velvet feel of the cape. The stinging in my eyes. My heart was thumping so loudly I could barely hear her words. I couldn't make sense of anything.

"I watched you and John that day," she said, in obvious pain. "Take my baby out of me like John took the little horse."

"No, you'll be fine," I assured her. "No one will hurt your baby."

"They will. Hector said come to cabin. Wear party robe and necklace. Then, she...said... 'sacrifice baby later.' I didn't know what..." Her breath shuddered. "Meant...until I saw...book. Take baby out of me like John took little horse. Keep it safe... from them."

I felt myself tremble. She who? "Just hang on."

"Hide baby," she said as her hand went limp. I put my finger on her neck. No pulse. I put my palm under her nose. No breath. I knew I had only seconds to make a decision.

Blair's head bobbed up and down like one of those little plastic dogs you see in the back of car windows. "Do it," she said. Her hair hung forward, nearly covering her face. Paler than the moon, she looked deranged sitting on her knees with her heels tucked under her butt, naked except for the open blouse, Mandy's blood pooling around her.

"She's dead," I said numbly.

"Then, do it."

And then, Blair howled. A ghastly unnerving sound. She rocked back and forth, sobbing. "I killed her. I didn't mean to!" she wailed, as she wrung the hem of Mandy's cloak between her hands. I had no idea what she meant and no time to deal with it now.

I ran to Blair's car and took the dagger out of the backseat, the one that had been launched at her. As I ran back, I seriously thought I was crazy for what I was about to do. Bees buzzed in my stomach, chased by a roiling serpent. I knelt by Mandy. Her soft eyes, now unconcerned, stared at me. I took a deep breath and bared her abdomen. I braced the knife's edge against one of her hipbones and drug its sharp point across her belly to the other hipbone. I was careful not to go too deep. Blair fainted when I pushed my hands into Mandy's abdomen and lifted out a baby boy.

Except for movies at the shelter, I had never seen a baby new from the womb. Such a small bundle, covered with its mother's blood and something that looked like wax.

I saw my hands move, but it was like they were someone else's hands. From somewhere, instructions came into my head and my hands followed them. I laid the baby on Mandy's chest and wiped him with a piece of the robe, as I had seen John do to the little horse. Maybe because I had caught bits and pieces of Aunt Angela's movies about what to expect at birth, I felt led to wipe out the baby's mouth, pat its back, and spank its feet. I consciously didn't remember seeing those things, but they seemed right, so I did them. Through some miracle, he took a breath. Then, he cried. Then, he wailed. I took some of the leather cord off the crucifix and tied it on either side of the umbilical cord and cut it.

Blair came to little by little. A look of sanity returned to her. Her eyes dried. She licked drool off her lips and rubbed her sleeve across her nose. She sniffed a big shuddering sniff. "Well, if she wasn't dead then, she is now," she remarked. She removed her blouse, laid it across her bare arms, and extended her arms to me. I handed the baby to her, wrapping him as best I could in her blouse. She pulled his small body to her. "That was freakin' amazing," she said.

I was thinking it was more like freakin' awful. "She was dead," I said. "I'm really sure she was dead," I repeated.

"She was dead," parroted Blair.

Someone had hit Mandy and left her to die. She was off the road, so someone had to have hauled her and the bike into this field.

The baby? Did I do that right? He seemed to be okay, but what should I do now? "Blair, do you have your cell phone?" I had to say it twice before she took her eyes from the baby and focused on me.

"It's in the glove compartment," she said. I left her kneeling by Mandy's body, gently rocking. Darkwater stood vigil.

Raphael followed me to the car, bleating like a goat gone mad. I put him in the backseat with Horatio and popped open the glove compartment. Calling 911 wasn't going to help Mandy now. I certainly wasn't on good terms with Buster. If he found us like this, he'd probably shoot me first and ask questions later. For all I knew, he was in on the sacrifice thing with Billy. No telling where Aunt Angela was, but no doubt she was surrounded by Ruby's relatives where she'd have a lot of explaining to do if she had to cut and run to me. I did what I had wanted to do all my life whenever I got in trouble, but never could. I called John.

I remembered he'd said he was always at Blessed Sacrament Church at the AA meeting on Friday evenings. I called information and had them dial the number. A monotone voice answered, "This is Harry. Blessed Sacrament Church. Jesus Saves. How can I help you?" I asked for John. After chair scuffling and coughing noises, John came on the line and I told him what went down. Maybe thirty minutes later, his old Cadillac pulled up by Blair's car. Not far behind him was Toni, coming from the other direction and out of breath from running, but covering ground fast to get to us.

"Holy shit," was Toni's take on the situation. Blair still knelt on the ground naked, rocking the baby. I was standing over Mandy in my swim top and jeans, covered in blood. A knife lay in blood pooled on the ground by Mandy's body. I thought Toni pretty much nailed it.

John came at me with his arms out. My knees buckled and I fell against him. His embrace was like salvation. He was strong and solid and smelled good. "I got you," he said. I could tell the warning I'd given John on the phone hadn't prepared him for the shock of the reality of Mandy lying dead on the ground. For a moment he didn't say a word. Then big waves of grief rolled off him, evident in sobs and tears. We clung together, holding each other up with every bit of strength we possessed. Toni came over and embraced us both. I looked through my tears into her eyes, wishing I could read humans like I could animals.

She walked over to Blair and helped her stand. They both looked at the baby. Blair handed the baby to Toni as if she were handing her a grenade. "Careful. No, do it this way," Blair instructed. "Put your hand under his head here. Cup his butt like this. Oh, you're not doing it right," she said.

Toni handed the baby to John then turned to me. "This is

awful," she whispered. "I'm so sorry for Mandy." A tear, shiny as mercury in the moonlight, slithered down her cheek and splashed on my hand, which I realized was holding onto her arm.

Patiently, John let Blair instruct him, too. Then she seemed to wilt a little. "I'm sorry. I, uh, I'm an idiot. Mandy was, after all, your daughter. And this baby is your grandson."

John took a deep breath. "I'll bury Mandy," he said. "I'll tell her aunt what happened and about the Devil People wanting this baby. She trusts me. She'll go off in that old trailer of hers and I'll tell people Mandy went with her. She won't be missed for a while."

We all looked at the tiny bundle in his arms. "What about him?" Blair asked.

"I'll take him to Madeline," John said. "She has plenty of milk for her baby and my grandson. They'll be safe at my place until we know who we can trust."

I must have looked like I felt. Scared to death.

Toni hugged my shoulder. "This is the right thing to do," she said. "If these crazies are after this baby, the best thing to do is hide him until you know who you're dealing with. Could be people in very high places."

The expression in John's swollen eyes moved from brooding to something darker as he looked at Toni standing there in a black robe. "This is on you," he said.

Toni just nodded and folded her arms around me as if to comfort me, but John pushed her away and pulled me to his own chest alongside the baby. "Get your ass back," he said.

A whinny caused both John and me to turn. Darkwater stood a few feet away. John hugged me tighter as the stallion reared up and ran into the night.

Chapter Sixteen

How would I pull off acting normal at today's wedding?

I'd slept fitfully, maybe fifteen minutes at a time. The dreams were bad enough, but each time I'd awaken, I'd remember Mandy was dead. Events of the night before would wash over me, threatening to drown me in grief.

Toni lay in bed beside me. John had dropped her off on the highway on his way to the Rez, and she'd walked the rest of the way to the ranch. She had shimmied up the tree to the porch roof and knocked softly on the window, looking into my tear-filled eyes with her puppy dog stare. I didn't want to, but God help me, I let her in. I couldn't resist the craving in my skin to just have another person hold me. Throughout the night, she woke up every time I woke up. I cried into her shoulder, talked to her once again about how awful death was, how unfair. She'd gotten me through the night, whispering comforting words, holding me. I finally fell into a deep sleep as the sun was coming up, making lemon-colored streaks across our bodies.

I awoke and watched her abdomen rise and fall for awhile. Then I put my feet on the floor about the same time a headache with claws attacked. I'd never again smirk at the girls at the shelter who said they couldn't get out of bed because of a migraine.

The clock on the night table seemed to tick, "Mandy's dead, Mandy's dead," as I trudged to the bathroom, put toothpaste on a brush and lathered up. I'd have to tell lies through these teeth all day about how happy I was for the lucky couple. I hoped they wouldn't fall out from all the lies before the day was over. I spat into the sink, opened the medicine cabinet and chugged down a couple of Advil. Hope to God no one pressed me too hard about anything. I would puke.

I clicked on the TV, volume on whisper so as not to wake Toni. A *Murder She Wrote* rerun was on. I couldn't follow the story line because of all the stuff in my own head. Had I made a mistake not telling the authorities? Maybe. Was I a murderer? Probably. But I knew if Mandy wasn't already dead when I took the baby, she couldn't have survived more than a few minutes with blood pumping out of her like that. Certainly not long enough for us to get her to a hospital. I knew I wouldn't have done it any different.

I didn't think anyone except Billy would be following up on what happened to Mandy anytime soon. The story that she left town with her aunt was highly believable, because it was their pattern to come and go about every few months or so. Ruby would miss Mandy doing the cleaning, but she wouldn't be alarmed. And Buster wouldn't follow up on Mandy's disappearance even if Billy wanted that. Buster would consider himself lucky Mandy was gone and leave it at that.

I tried to remember the facts. Had I had forgotten anything relevant? Mandy had been wearing one of those robes when we found her, but I felt sure she hadn't made it to the coven meeting I interrupted by the lake. If Mandy had been there when Blair and I were making a ruckus, she would've taken off her hood and shown herself to me right away.

When we'd found Mandy, she'd had an upside down crucifix around her neck made of shiny black beads, attached to a black leather cord. I was sure she hadn't known the significance of the inverted crucifix.

Why had she been out on that road on the scooter? Had Billy been with her at the cabin after all and frightened her and she tried to run away? But, I hadn't seen his truck. Maybe one of the other Satanists had run her down. That didn't make sense. I had read on the Internet that a ritual sacrifice infant is supposed to be perfect. They wouldn't have wanted to chance hurting the baby until it was time to sacrifice it.

Poor Mandy. My heart ached at the loss of my sister. My only comforting thought was of the child. He was beautiful and safe. I wondered how he was doing. I was sure John would contact me soon, after he buried Mandy in the land of her ancestors. Unless John told, no one would ever find out where he buried her. According to John, Pine Ridge Reservation had as many secrets as it had tumbleweeds.

Toni stirred and opened her eyes. She held out her arms to me and I joined her on the bed. "How you feeling?" she asked.

"I feel like crap," I said. "But I'll be okay. Having you with me last night helped more than you'll ever know." I hugged her tight. "Please say I haven't invited a card-carrying devil worshipper into my bed."

"I haven't invited a card car—"

I grabbed her hair and pulled. "You better not be lying! How am I supposed to be cheerful today? To face a wedding full of smiling faces? That may be harder than getting through last night."

"Ow!" She pulled my hand away from her hair and rubbed her scalp. "I get the picture. You're strong. Now about today. You'll be okay. At least I don't think you'll be seeing Billy. I doubt he has the guts to face you after the fiasco by the lake."

"Right. He has to know I would have recognized those boots of his."

"I'll protect you from Billy," said Toni. "My dad taught me some of the moves he learned in Special Forces. I'll turn his junk to pudding if I have to," she said, and flexed her arm muscles for me, making us both laugh.

"Yeah, I'm lucky you're such a bruiser," I said and patted her skinny ass. I looked at the bedside clock. "It's almost four in the afternoon! I can't believe it's that late. I better get a move on. The wedding is in a couple hours."

The Advil was doing its magic. My head felt better. Ruby, ever the wonderful hostess even though this was her big day, had left a basket of scones and jelly outside the door with a thermos of coffee. Toni and I shared them in bed and also the one coffee cup. We sneaked down the corridor to the bathroom and showered together, soaping and rinsing off the negative energy of what we'd seen together the night before.

I worked myself into a light blue sheath dress from Blair's closet as Toni put on her jeans and T-shirt. I was pulling a brush through my hair when I heard a knock. Toni kissed me goodbye and silently let herself out the window.

I opened the door. Aunt Angela stood there, wearing a pale gray silk pantsuit with an abalone necklace that reflected blues, pinks and grays. Blair stood beside her. Crap. I had wanted to tell Aunt Angela about finding the necklace and Buster's suspicions about me. I didn't want Blair to hear any of it. She looked freaky enough. One more stress might push her into hysteria.

I put on my game face. "Aunt Angela, you're a stunner," I said, motioning them in. "You too, Blair." I stood in front of a mirror putting finishing touches on my makeup.

"Don't I know it." Aunt Angela gave me a tired smile as little lines of fatigue played at the corners of her eyes. She and Blair sat on the bed. Blair was silent.

"You look pretty great yourself," Aunt Angela said.

"Makeup can do wonders," I said, as I reached for some concealer I found in the bathroom for my under eye area. Aunt Angela stood and picked it up after I placed it on the dresser. She looked over my shoulder into the mirror and patted some under her own eyes.

"It's not about us today, is it?" she said. "This is about two middle-aged people staring into each other's eyes like they don't see the wrinkles and promising to spend the rest of their lives loving only each other. I'm happy for my big brother."

"Me, too," I said, and gave her a hug. Colin had been a butt wipe to us in the past, but he didn't seem to be that same person now.

The sound of honeybees and chirping birds accompanied us to the car. I worried that if Blair and I were silent, Aunt Angela would figure something was up, so I tried hard to overcome my malaise and make small talk. She relieved us of the responsibility of talking by dominating the conversation herself. She was full of news. What fun Ruby was. How great she looked. The trip to Mt. Rushmore. Some Indian art she bought. Blair and I nodded, occasionally stealing wary looks at one another.

Little pinpricks of moisture rose on my upper lip as we entered the church. I took a deep breath of scented air as a smiling usher escorted us to a pew adorned with pink ribbon and little white flowers. Aunt Angela slid in, then me. Blair followed, bumping into my hipbone as she pushed into the polished pew beside me, making way for the person beside her. My arm brushed against the ivory satin ribbon tied around her waist. She was decked out in a dress almost as lacy and white as a bride's dress. She looked beautiful and vulnerable, and for the first time in my life I felt sorry for her that she loved Billy and would probably never have a wedding like this of her own.

"Darkwater didn't come home," Blair whispered to me. "Daddy was fit to be tied. I was about to tell him everything when he said it was probably his fault because Darkwater's stall latch had been loose. He blamed himself for not fixing it when he should have. I let him believe it was his fault. I'm on my way to hell, anyway."

I nodded. We both were.

Holding a Bible, Reverend Ardis Chance stood in vestments and clerical collar at the front of the church under a flowery arch of pink roses. Dust motes danced in the air around her slumped shoulders. Her face had the same ashen hue as her hair.

"She looks like death on a cracker," Aunt Angela whispered to me as Ardis opened the Bible and stared at the congregation over her glass rims. Did I see her sway a little?

Organ music came from somewhere and seemed to give Ardis some starch. One of Ruby's little nieces walked down the aisle, scattering rose petals. Billy stepped from behind a curtain at the front of the church with Colin. *Billy was Colin's best man.* I felt Blair stiffen beside me as she grabbed my hand

and squeezed.

Ruby and Colin looked splendid, she in a pale pink beaded suit and pillbox hat with veil and he in a black western cut suit, crisp white shirt and black bolo tie. They beamed at each other as they read the vows they each had written. Something about he would and she would and each other was the Fourth of July, cotton candy and Disneyland all rolled into one. Then, Ardis went blah, blah, blah, God's will, something, something. I couldn't retain it. My eyes were on Billy. His eyes were on Blair. After vows were said and songs were sung by Little Elvis, the smiling couple marched down the aisle to the steps outside. Billy and the bridal party followed. The rest of us trailed out, throwing rice.

"Birds are gonna die," said Blair as she looked down at the sidewalk. "They'll eat the rice and their stomachs will swell up and they'll explode. I read it in a book."

She looked far too somber. "That's not true," I said, not knowing if it was or not. "Smile," I whispered as we made our way to the 'Stang. I patted her back hoping her mood would take a turn for the better.

"What's wrong?" Aunt Angela asked Blair.

"Where shall I start?" said Blair.

"Her stomach's a little upset," I said. "Would you mind too much riding over with one of the relatives? We'll be along later." Maybe Blair needed to talk it out.

"No problem," said Aunt Angela. "I'll get a ride over with Tula and Ed."

We dropped Aunt Angela with Ed and Tula and headed out. As we came to a stoplight, Blair signaled a left turn heading back toward the ranch.

"No, Blair. I think we have to make an appearance at the reception," I said. "We have to make things look as normal as possible. People will think something is weird if we don't go."

"Fine," Blair said through gritted teeth and turned her right signal on. My mouth felt like I'd been sucking on a wool blanket. I pointed to a McDonald's drive-through and we turned in. She ordered a couple Cokes.

"You want to talk about it, Blair?" I asked.

"I'd rather not," she said.

I asked, "What did you mean last night when you said you had killed Mandy?" I asked.

She swallowed, and tears spilled down her cheeks. "She wouldn't have been on the road if I'd given her a ride to the lake like she asked. She said she wanted to be a 'member of the club,' too. I didn't want her there, and I told her no. I figured that was the end of it, but I guess she tried to ride the scooter there and got killed by someone who didn't see her."

"Or maybe by Billy, who did it intentionally on his way to Satanfest," I said.

"You're crazy. Billy wasn't at the lake that night."

"Sure, he was," I said. "I saw his boots. Nobody else has boots like that."

"Hey, things happened fast. Maybe you saw boots that were similar to Billy's. I know Billy. He would never be involved in anything that would hurt Mandy, or animals."

"Yeah, just like everybody knew OJ was too famous to commit murder," I said.

Blair gave me a scathing look. "I feel better now," she said. "Let's go to the reception."

By the time we got there, the band had people up and dancing the hokey pokey. Ruby was giggling while Colin showed off his skill with his shiny quick draw pistols. Little Elvis and other kids were jumping and swatting at crepe paper bells hanging in the doorways.

An arm slid around my waist. "Let's dance," Billy said. "Save a dance for me, Blair?" he said over his shoulder as he spun me onto the floor.

"God knows I don't want to talk to you," he said. "But I need to know. Have you seen Mandy?" He pulled me into a vise-like grip.

"Me?" I squeaked.

"Blair told me you were trying to persuade Mandy to go to that unwed mothers' home your aunt runs." He gave me a frosty look. "You didn't put her on a plane, did you?"

"I wish," I said.

"She's supposed to be here," he said. "I couldn't find her last night. I called the hospital and everywhere I could think she might be. Nothing. I told Dad she was missing, but he won't help look for her. Have you seen her?"

"I haven't seen her," I said. I pulled his hand from my waist with my finger and thumb, holding it like it was something rotten. "But if I do, I'll let her know you're looking for her so she can run the other way. I know what you want to do. I saw you."

He let me go and stepped back. "What are you talking about?"

"I know you want to sacrifice Mandy's baby. I know you're a member of the cult that's been killing the animals."

Anger hardened his jaw bone to rock. "I swear," he finally said, "you are so dumb, opposable thumbs are wasted on you. You may think I killed your mother. But, do you really believe that I would kill my own baby? You're a nutcase."

"If it were your baby," I said.

"Listen, you hate me. I get that. But interfering with what Mandy and I have is criminal. She needs me. So stop trying to come between us." He looked up. "By the way, heads-up. I see my father is here to bring Angela his regards."

I looked up. Buster came through the door with Deputy Cantwell. The music stopped, the crowd parted, and they moved across the room to where Aunt Angela was standing with Ruby and Colin.

"Angela McKee, I'm arresting you for the theft of a necklace from the home of Angus McKee. You have the right to remain silent..."

Even though I heard the words tumble out of his mouth, my brain took a moment to decipher them. It was not until I heard Ruby's voice that I realized what was happening.

"She ain't guilty all by herself, sheriff," said Ruby. "I can't let her take this on alone. I'm the one who unlocked the house so she could get in. So, it's me and Angie together that are guilty." All eyes turned toward Ruby.

"Shut up, Ruby," said Aunt Angela.

Buster leaned back on his heels and crossed his arms as Deputy Cantwell put the cuffs on Aunt Angela. "So you two were in this together," he said. "Cuff her, too."

As Deputy Cantwell made a move toward Ruby, Colin stepped forward. "Now, hold up a minute," he said. "That's crazy talk. Nobody is guilty of anything. My father has dementia. He doesn't remember that my mother gave that necklace to Angela years ago."

"Keep out of it, Colin," Buster said. "I have a complaint and I have to follow up. Let us do our job."

Little Elvis piped up. "No way, pig. You're not taking my auntie to jail!" That said, he pulled Colin's quick draw pistol from his holster. He waved it in front of Buster. Some of the guests gasped and stepped back.

The sheriff's lips tightened. "Now, kid, everybody knows that's just a show pistol and not loaded. I don't know what you think you're going do with that. Old Man McKee says he's a victim of theft and Ruby is involved, so she's coming with me. Colin, take care of that brat."

There was a loud report and flash. Seventy-five pounds of ice crumbled to the floor as a punch bowl and ice sculpture bit the dust. Purple punch rushed onto the floor. Deputy Cantwell sprang into action and grabbed the gun away from Elvis while Buster composed himself, then cuffed Ruby.

The crowd parted for the sheriff and deputy as they led Aunt Angela and Ruby away. Aunt Angela looked at the splotches of purple punch on her pantsuit and leveled her eyes at Elvis in a stern look. Little Elvis wailed. Ruby's hat and veil were cocked sideways on her head like a boat listing on a high sea. Her hands cuffed behind her, she kept blowing at her veil to try to straighten it. Colin, looking grim, trailed along to accompany Ruby to jail. Deputy Cantwell followed with teary-eyed Elvis and his sobbing mother.

Police cars gobbled up the prisoners. Deputy Cantwell slid behind the wheel of his patrol car to spirit Elvis and his mother away. Ruby and Aunt Angela were in the backseat of Buster's patrol car. I managed to lean in Buster's car window. "What proof do you have?" I demanded.

"None of your business," Buster said. "Just be glad you're in the clear. If you want to talk with the prisoners, come by the jail in an hour. You can ask them all about it yourself after we process them."

Billy came up behind me and squeezed me out to say something to his dad. He turned to me as Buster pulled away from the curb. "Angus called me last night," he said. "He's come to depend on me for various odd jobs since Colin's been so busy with the ranch. He was crowing like a rooster about how he'd found this Caitlen necklace and he wanted me to come by in the morning and take it to the bank when it opened to put in his safe deposit box. When I showed up, it was gone. He had it in his mind you stole it. I'd seen Angela parked inside the fence the night before when I was doing my normal property check for the old man. She was behind Angus's house. That didn't seem weird at the time. After all, she's his daughter. I thought maybe she was visiting the old coot. But later, Dad told me that Angus hasn't spoken to Angela in years. She was in Colin's truck, but I recognized her all right. She was just sitting there smoking, with the lights off, back in some trees. Then I saw her get out of the car and enter the house. And, I realized later, she had never turned on a light."

He smiled broadly at me. "When Angus told me about the theft, I realized I had to tell Dad about Angela. It was my civic duty. I would've loved to hang it on you. But if I'd tried, Angela would have confessed to clear you. Anyway, when I told Dad about Angela being there, he figured she took it. He told me he remembered she'd had a fit over it years ago when Angus threw her out. I didn't know Ruby was in on it, though."

"That's so flimsy it will never hold up," I said. "My aunt never stole anything in her life. She was probably out there smoking, getting some peace and quiet, waiting for Ruby or Mandy to give them a ride back to the Bonnie B."

"What about what Ruby said, that they did this together? Is she lying?" he asked.

"She probably just meant she accidentally forgot to set the alarm and left the door unlocked. After all, she's been preoccupied over this wedding. So she thinks it's her fault the robber got in. Since Buster thinks the thief is Aunt Angela, Ruby does, too. She feels partly responsible."

"Well, they can tell it to the judge," said Billy. "My advice to you is don't get in Dad's way. Believe me, he's not a man you want to get angry."

"Don't waste your concern." I gave him a haughty look. "When Colin contacts his attorney, he'll have Ruby and Aunt Angela out of jail in a heartbeat."

Billy's lips turned up ever so slightly at the corners "Oh, bad luck there. I mentioned to Judge Koop about how the fish are running in Tarrent Creek. He won't be back until after the weekend. Angela and Ruby will have each other for company until the judge can arraign them on Monday."

"You never miss an opportunity to complicate my life, do you?" I sneered at him.

"You haven't seen anything, yet. Despite you, I'll find Mandy. Keep in mind, I know where you live."

"Do your worst," I said, and tossed my head at him in defiance. As I turned, I tumbled over Blair who was on her hands and knees.

"What are you doing down there?" I yelped at her.

"Getting this rice up. People keep throwing it. So bad for the birds." She got to her knees with handfuls of rice and dumped it into her purse.

Billy reached down and helped her to her feet. "C'mon, Blair."

He grabbed Blair's keys from her purse and threw them at me. "You take Blair's 'Stang," he said. "Blair will be with me."

They left me sprawled on the sidewalk, Billy in the lead, holding her hand. Blair stumbled along behind Billy like a five-year-old. She looked back and gave me a quick wave.

Chapter Seventeen

I gave the heavy glass door of the Pell Mell City Jail a push and walked into a lobby where tiny windows at the top of tan cinder block walls allowed the only sunshine. Gunmetal gray chairs were lined up against the walls. An American flag and a South Dakota flag gave the room its only color.

Deputy Cantwell was striking keys on an ancient typewriter with his meaty fingers. He looked up as I approached, shoving in place a long strand of hair that he used to disguise his bald spot. A twelve cup coffee pot made a rude flushing sound as I sat down across the desk from him. The FBI's most wanted stared at me from the wall.

"Antitech?" I asked, nodding to the old typewriter.

"I guess. Buster tried to show me how to use the new computer system, but he's got no patience. His teaching consists mostly of yelling. So I brought this relic from home and unplugged the computer. He's still mad at me about that but my blood pressure has gone down lots. If he wants me to learn the system, he can damn well hire a tech guy to train me on it. C'mon back."

He stood and motioned me through a metal door. "We let Elvis go home with his mom and a promise of a good spanking." He hunched his shoulders. "Just an accident. Colin said he loaded the pistol a month ago. You know, he's been jumpy, what with losing his cattle to those damn devil lovers and all. Said he was nervous about the wedding and forgot to unload it. He's lucky that twerp didn't shoot anybody."

I was sure that in any other town Colin would have been charged with something, like endangering a child or having a loaded gun in an auditorium full of people, or whatever. In Pell Mell, it's good to be a buddy of the sheriff.

Deputy Cantwell led me down some steps to an area that contained three cells. It seemed, so far, to be a low crime weekend since two cells were empty. In the last cell Aunt Angela lay on a cot against a colorful quilt blanket, smoking and reading a magazine. Ruby was sitting in a rocking chair doing needlepoint and humming. A folded screen was propped against the wall for privacy while using a toilet by the bed. A bookcase held a few novels and magazines and a small tray with two candy bars. And, yes, by God, a doily. Mayberry RFD. I looked at Deputy Cantwell and he hunched his shoulders. "My idea," he said. "Ladies need a little extra care," he said.

Aunt Angela looked up. "Humdinger of a party, wasn't it?" she said, smiling.

I placed my hands on the bars between us. "You doing okay?" I asked.

"I am. We've only been here a couple hours, but to tell the truth this is a much needed rest. All this sightseeing with the relatives and all, it's been tiring." She let the magazine slide from her fingers to the concrete floor. "It feels good to lay here and nap and read. They brought us a delicious meal, too. The deputy said Mrs. Cantwell cooked it for us." She gave him a smile. "And the deputy was decent enough to let me have my smokes. So, yeah, doing fine." She looked at Ruby. "How about you, Ruby?"

"I'm enjoying your company, dear Angela. I been dang tuckered myself. Getting this wedding together—whew! Tired to death, in fact. I really need this rest to prepare for, you know, a rigorous wedding night." She blushed.

I know I must've looked at them like they were a couple space aliens. Everybody's worried to death and these two act like they're spending time at La Dee Dah Spa. I folded my arms across my chest and wondered if I'd get so old and tired that a weekend in jail sounded like a good idea. "You'll probably only be here a couple days. No longer than that. Buster's really got no case."

"Now, there's a man with a heart as black as a crow's wing," said Aunt Angela. "If it weren't for that deputy of his, we'd probably still be in cuffs. He had those cuffs on so tight, they pinched. No use bellyaching, though. Thanks to Colin, I know everything is going to be okay. There's a chair by the wall. Sit down, River. I have something I need to tell you."

Aunt Angela lit up another cigarette. I seated myself, tipped the chair back, and propped my feet on the bars. "Shoot," I said.

"River, I have breast cancer," she said. "That's why I've been avoiding you since we got here. That's why I haven't been answering your calls. I didn't want you to find out and I knew if I spent much time around you, I'd eventually just blab it out. It was all I could do not to tell you in the airplane."

Whump! I swear, that's the sound I heard coming from my chest. I put my feet flat on the floor and popped straight up into a sitting position. "What did the doctor say? How bad is it?" I asked.

She waved a hand at my concern. "It's fine. Prognosis is good, with treatment." She looked into my eyes as if pleading for understanding. "'Course, I have to quit these things," she said, looking at her cigarette like she was already missing it. "When I got the phone call about the cancer after the wedding invitation showed up, I decided to use the opportunity to come here and find the necklace and take it. I have no health insurance. No way to pay for the treatments I need. That necklace meant my survival."

Ruby said, "I didn't know about Angela's cancer. I thought she wanted the necklace simply because her mother wanted her to have it. If I'd known the real reason, Colin and I would've given her the money for her treatments and we could have spared her this. But, I didn't know. So, when Angus told me he'd found the necklace, I told Angie where he put it. All I had to do was leave the door unlocked and the security system off when I left. Angie did the rest. I didn't feel a moment's guilt about it, either."

"Of course you didn't," said Aunt Angela. "By rights, that necklace is mine. When Angus kicked me out he didn't even give me time to pack a bag, he was so furious." She shook her head. "What a scene it was! He was hitting me and Mother was crying. Mom called me at Mickey's place a couple days later to tell me she'd been forbidden to see me but she wanted me to have the necklace. It was a bold step for her to call. Poor Mom. She was never very bold when it came to standing up to Angus."

Ruby piped up. "Well, he beat her, I'll bet. Can you blame her for trying to keep him calm? She never even learned to drive, poor thing. That old man gave the Buttrams more liberty than he gave her."

"The Buttrams?" Aunt Angela said. "Oh, yes. The caretakers back then. They at least got paid and could come and go as they pleased. Mom would have been better off if Angus had hired her instead of marrying her. He had all Mother's assets put in his name. She knew I'd never see a penny. That necklace was the only thing she owned by herself. Momma didn't want Angus's attorney to handle the transfer of the necklace to me because she didn't trust him not to give it to Angus. So, she hid it and said she'd get it to me somehow."

Aunt Angela tapped ash from her cigarette. "I think the stress of the whole thing got to her. She died of a heart attack before she could do that. I blame Angus. At her funeral I stared holes in that old man's back. But he never once looked at me."

The three of us were silent a minute, I think each reflecting on how anyone could be so mean as Angus McKee. "Ruby," I said, "why didn't you just take the necklace for Aunt Angela once you found it, since you knew it was intended for her?"

Ruby put her needlepoint down. "Oh my, I couldn't actually

have taken anything like that. It wasn't mine. That would be stealing. But I didn't see the harm in leaving the door unlocked and leaving the security system off so Angela could get what was rightfully hers in the first place."

I shook my head. The moral distinction escaped me.

Aunt Angela threw her cigarette into the toilet bowl. "It pained me, but I pried the jewels out of the cross so they would be harder to trace. I put them in a plastic container and put the container in the freezer at the ranch. Ruby and I thought it would be the perfect hiding place. But now we can't find the jewels." She and Ruby looked at each other, shook their heads, and looked sad.

I let my head fall forward and rolled it around on my shoulders. "Doesn't that just figure," I said. "I knew when you made me come out here, it would be the death of us both."

"Oh, don't turn drama queen on me," said Aunt Angela. "I'm glad we came. Colin, for the first time, is trying to be a good guy. No offense, Ruby."

"None taken," said Ruby. "I can't fault you blaming him for what he did before he found the Lord."

"He left not long before you showed up, River," said Aunt Angela. "When I told him about the cancer, he said he would pay for my treatments. 'Course I don't want to accept his money, but I don't have much choice. It's a big load off my mind that I can get the treatments I need, whether I ever see those jewels again or not."

A nasty thought hit me. I'd been so preoccupied the day I cleaned the kitchen. Had I tossed the jewels without realizing it when I cleaned out the freezer? As I got up to leave, guilt colored my face. I thought about all the laws I'd broken in the last twenty-four hours and how I belonged in jail and not them. I blew them both a kiss as I left.

I sat in the parking lot awhile before I kicked myself in gear. The sun was just now going down, but I wanted to go to the ranch, crawl into bed and hide under the covers. I wondered if Toni was there, waiting. But I was also concerned about Blair being with Billy. It would be just like him to blow her off and leave her stranded somewhere.

I drove to the Masonic Lodge to check on her. Billy's truck was still there.

A few other cars were in the lot. Some of Ruby's relatives were carrying out folding chairs and loading them in a truck when I walked inside the lodge. It appeared the party had carried on for awhile without the guests of honor, but now the party was over. The boys in the band were putting away instruments and gathering up electrical cords. The relatives were clearing tables of crystal dishes and tablecloths. Samantha Peet swept broken glass into a dustpan. She looked up and waved, then followed me into the kitchen to throw the glass into a trash can. Wonder of wonders, Blair was there washing dishes. Billy was nowhere to be seen.

I couldn't believe that with his money Colin hadn't hired catering and cleanup. Money meant a lot to Colin, and he had shown he was pretty tight with it. Yet he had offered it to Aunt Angela without hesitation. Maybe he had changed. And, Blair, doing dishes? Ruby had certainly shaken things up in that family. "You guys need any help?" I asked.

"We're okay," said Blair. "You hungry?" She motioned toward a table full of food. "We've got leftovers."

"No thanks. I could use a glass of punch," I said, reaching for a glass from a tray of already poured glasses full of pink liquid and chugging it down like a dehydrated runner. "I came back to see if you need a ride, Blair."

"No, and don't wait for me," she said in a firm tone. "I'll get a ride with Billy when I'm done here." I opened my mouth and she put her hand up. "Don't bother to argue. I'm a big girl and I trust Billy." She took my glass and tossed it into sudsy water.

Samantha must have noticed me bite my lip, because she said, "Let me give you a ride when we're through here, Blair. Billy's busy taking down the stage and hauling chairs away. No telling when he'll get done." To me she said, "Ruby and Angela okay?" She picked up another glass of punch from the tray and handed it to me.

"They're good. They'll be out of jail soon. Buster's got no case," I replied as I took a gulp and set the drink down.

"Good," Samantha said. "I like Buster, but sometimes he's a

little over the top."

"Not to mention underhanded," I said. "Not a quality I admire in people."

She blushed. I had no idea what Buster had on her to make her lie about what she'd seen when Mom died, but I felt she got my point. I turned and made my way to the door. Too late, I spied a shiny piece of ice sticking out from under the toe of my shoe just as I stepped down. I slipped, almost doing the splits before catching myself. Sticky punch blessed my blouse, and I pulled a groin muscle. Terrific.

Samantha inquired from across the room if I needed help. I waved her off, and limped across the parking lot to Blair's car. I laid my head against the steering wheel and closed my eyes. I thought of Mandy's still, dead face. I rolled down the window and took a few gulps of night air and saw Billy step outside. He saw me and walked toward the 'Stang. I pulled out and headed back to the ranch.

The grandfather clock chimed 11:00 p.m. as I stepped into the kitchen at the Bonnie B. The house was still and dark. Thank goodness no one had bothered to lock the back door. Colin had probably left it unlocked for me, or Ed and Tula. The nightly news was on the TV in the great room, but I didn't see anyone watching it. I picked up the remote and hit the off button, took off my shoes and headed to the staircase. That was the last coherent thought I had for awhile.

I had anticipated that the stairs would be difficult to climb with the pulled muscle, but I was curiously without pain. In fact, I don't remember climbing the stairs. It was as if I floated up. As I passed the room adjoining mine, I heard soft snoring. The end of a busy day for Tula and Ed. I thought it weird that it seemed to take a long time to pass their bedroom door, like time was made of taffy.

I was so tired that I didn't change my clothes. I crawled onto the bed and drifted, not asleep, but not quite awake. Thinking that I couldn't move if I tried, it didn't seem to bother me much. My body, bound in some sort of invisible cocoon, seemed to be floating. My last thought before I slept was that Randall, the bad guy serpentine monster from the movie *Monsters, Inc.*, came out of the closet.

Soft, foot shuffling noises. Whispers. Sensory input somehow making its way into my brain. Someone had hold of my feet.

A deep voice surfaced in the darkness. "Want I should conk her on the head?"

"No. Looks like the Ketamine did the trick," said a voice that sounded like Toni's.

"Good. I wasn't sure if I got enough from Jerry's."

I could hear them as if I were under water and they weren't. No matter how I tried, I couldn't swim to the top. Was I inside Blair's snow globe? Or, not snow? Was it feathers? Floating down to cover my eyes. Eyes everywhere. Cats' eyes bobbing around. Sweet. Pretty. Here, kitty, kitty. A knife? How sharp and shiny. A really pretty knife.

"We just want to scare her," said Toni Voice. "Maybe whack her hair off. Just so she knows we can get to her whenever we want."

"No. I'm supposed to do her," said Deep Voice.

"Hector, I'm sure we're just supposed to scare her."

"I'm sure Cleopatra said do," responded the voice of Hector. "Or, at least take a finger. But here, hold the knife while I get my cell."

"Man, quit wiping your boogers on this knife," said Toni. "It's disgusting."

"Shut up. Hey. No. Not you. Listen. Are we supposed to take a finger off this bitch or cut her heart out? Stop that!"

"Stop what?" asked Toni.

"Whatever you're doing. Okay. She says do. Get the heart."

"We'd better take her out of here, man, to do the deed," said Toni. "Don't wanna wake the Fudstones on the other side of the wall and we don't wanna be leaving evidence. I watch CSI. They can get you with a thread, man. Let's take her out to the barn. That way we can set a fire after and burn the evidence. Here, you get her legs and I'll take her arms and we'll take her out the window onto the roof. Then, I'll lower her down to you."

"Hey, stop that!" said Hector.

"Stop what?" asked Toni.

"Hey, quit it." Hector again.

"Not me, man. Man, what is that?" asked Toni.

"These things are bats! Bats! Shit, everywhere."

"Shit, I'm bleeding," said Toni.

"I'm out of here," said Hector.

For a few moments, the only thing I heard was scuffling sounds. Then, silence. Then, someone blew in my ear. "Sleep, little snake chaser. These young badasses will not bother you."

I opened my eyes. Uncle Charley pulled a coverlet made of stars and night sky up to my chin. He pulled a pouch from his shirt pocket and sprinkled tobacco around my bed. His old head was haloed by snowy white hair. Wisps of it touched my chin as he leaned in to plant a kiss on my cheek. I felt wonderful, watching Uncle Charley and his bats float around the bed.

I woke next morning feeling a little groggy. As daylight spilled into the room, I stretched and yawned, trying not to look for tobacco on the bed. It was like trying not to sneeze. I looked. Of course, there wasn't any.

I must really have had Toni on the brain, to dream her up weird like that. But why dream that she was trying to take my heart? Symbolism, I supposed.

Despite the dream, I really felt better than I had a right to. After all, I was captive in the place I hated most in the world. Cult members could retaliate at any time. But suspicion of being a jewel thief was no longer my burden, and the news that Aunt Angela would get medical care buoyed me. And there was the baby. How was the baby? I hadn't heard from John.

I showered, put my hair in a ponytail and slipped on jeans and a T-shirt. I tiptoed past Tula's room down the stairs to the kitchen. My groin muscle was giving me a fit and I rubbed it as I backed into the kitchen door and gave it a push with my butt. When the door opened, I tripped over a toaster.

"Good grief!" I exclaimed. Colin stood by the sink, his shirt half tucked in, his hair uncombed. "Colin, whatever are you doing?" It looked like the kitchen had blown up. Every cabinet door stood open. Colin had pulled out every can, bottle and automatic gadget he could find and put them on the counter top and floor.

"I'm trying to find those damn jewels," he said, through

gritted teeth. "According to Angie, they couldn't have left this room. She thought she put them in the freezer, but I didn't find them. I've searched everywhere, including the breadmaker—" He held up an appliance. "This is a bread maker, right?"

"Yes, it is," I said, trying to keep panic out of my voice. "Listen, Uncle Colin, I have something I need to confess." I would rather have kissed King Kong than to admit this to Colin, but I couldn't stand this guilt any longer. "I may have thrown out those jewels by mistake when I cleaned out the refrigerator." I sank back into myself and waited for the tidal wave of shit that was surely headed my way. I could feel blood rushing up my neck into my face. "Uh, I'm sorry," I stammered. "Really. Really. Sorry."

He reached into his pocket and pulled out his handkerchief and blew his nose. "No, River, I'm sorry," he said. "I know I haven't been the nicest uncle. It's no wonder you're standing there trembling."

He put his arm around my shoulders. "Briana would be so ashamed of me. I should've taken you in and raised you for my own. But, John and I, well, we were at crosshairs. I was wrong. It wasn't your fault. Never you." We were quiet for a moment as we leaned against the kitchen counter. "Not the easiest thing to come out here and face me after all this time, huh?"

"Not so much, no."

He shut his eyes and hung his head, then jerked his head up. "Amen," he said. "I've turned it over to the Lord. If we're supposed to find those jewels, the Lord will provide them." Then he got busy again looking through the kitchen.

Could Blair have discovered the jewels and hid them for her New York expenses? I went to her bedroom and gave it a thorough search. I looked under the bed, behind the nooks, the crannies. When I looked in the closet, I saw the small amount of clothing I had brought alongside the lovely clothes that Blair had let me wear. She had about a million pairs of shoes and purses to match. I looked in every one. Nothing.

When I returned to the kitchen, Uncle Colin looked up from an open drawer with a Twinkie in his hand. He thrust it into his pocket. "Breakfast," he said. "I sure do miss Ruby's cooking. Well, I guess I'll go back to the lawyer's office then and see what magic he can work to get the girls out. Judge Koop came back early from fishing, according to Buster. Maybe I can talk sense to him."

"Uncle Colin." I said, "Again, I'm really sorry."

He hugged me. "Have faith in the Lord. It'll all turn out like it should."

We both jumped when the vibrate and wail went off on his cell phone. He fished it out of his pocket, and did a lot of head nodding, frowning, whistling, and an "I'll get back to you."

"That was Buster with good news and bad news. He said the doctor at Rapid City General called him, saying he'd found jewels in Tula's gut. Seems her and Ed had just left town when she got terrible pain and they headed straight for the hospital. Evidently, she ate 'em during one of her sleepwalking food orgies."

"That is good news," I said. "Is she okay?"

"Yes, she'll be fine. The bad news is now Ruby and Angela are incriminated but good because Tula says she couldn't have eaten them anywhere else but here." He paused and ran his hand through a piece of my hair. "What's this in your hair? Tobacco?"

Chapter Eighteen

I left Colin and walked from the kitchen in a kind of daze and plunked down on the couch. I had felt pretty good when I got up, but now with the news of the noose tightening around Aunt Angela's neck, I went into a funk. I reached for the remote and clicked on the TV to distract myself from worrying, and became aware of two things. *Batman* was the movie of the week. And, Toni had been in my room last night and wanted me dead. As it all came rushing back, I inhaled so deep my stomach flattened itself against my backbone.

I've strayed into an alternate universe, I thought—one where people say they care about you then try to kill you. No, wait. That's this universe—at least according to the movies I see on Lifetime TV. But this—this was off my personal chart of expected experiences. I hadn't seen it coming. How can a person cup your butt so fondly and then in the same week plan your murder? I didn't know, but I knew I hadn't been dreaming. I ran after Colin. He was getting into his truck when I caught him. "Is

Billy supposed to be working at the Bonnie B today?" I asked.

He blew into a hankie and wiped his nose. "Let me think... No, I gave him the day off. He may be at the lake, moving back into his cabin. I told him he could live there while he worked for me, but I think he gave it up for one of the wedding guests." He paused as he put the hankie in his pocket. "You might try the parsonage first." He started the truck. "Why do you want to talk with Billy? Have you two made peace?" The diesel engine growled around his words.

"Not really." I didn't want to tell Uncle Colin the real reason I wanted to see Billy was to beat answers out of him about the cult and Toni. "I just wanted to ask him if he'd had any leads on Darkwater," I offered as an excuse.

"I doubt it. I'm sure he'd let me know first thing if he did. I hope you two bury the hatchet."

"We're speaking, at least." I didn't want to go into any of this with him.

"Good. Don't worry about straightening the kitchen," Uncle Colin said. "This is Mandy's day to come in and clean. Well, I'm off. I need to take care of this thing with Ruby and Ang." He waved as he pulled away.

I watched him drive away. "Mandy won't be in today," I said quietly to myself. A dust devil swirled around my feet as I walked to the house, pushing leaves into the kitchen when I opened the screen door and scattering them across the floor.

I put away everything that had been torn out of the cabinets and wiped down the counters, along with the refrigerator and stove. I dropped a wet towel on the floor and swirled it around with my foot to get some jelly stains up and dumped the towel in the washer. This was the first time I could remember not being soothed by cleaning.

I made a breakfast tray with a scrambled ham and egg quickie, wheat toast and a diet soda and headed out to the pool house. I picked a flower off one of the bushes as I passed and put it on the tray.

The pool house was hardly more than a shed. I opened the door and nearly tripped over one of those foam tubular pool toys. I was surprised that Ruby would insist Blair stay out here and was a little touched that Blair would put up with it. Ruby's tough love had certainly rocked Princess Blair's world.

Blair lay on a cot in a corner under a window, a black sleeping mask over her eyes, snoring with her mouth open. Waking her might be like poking a bear with a stick, but it was nearly ten in the morning. I had things to do and Billy to confront. I sat the tray on a packing crate that said Aqua Perfect Pool Supplies on the side. "Wake up, sleepyhead," I said.

"Ulemumphelump," she said and rolled over. I rubbed the cold can of soda pop against the sole of her foot.

"What the…" She awoke, arms flailing and legs kicking, and whisked the mask off her eyes.

"Have some breakfast," I said and offered her a piece of toast. She took it out of my hand and threw it at me.

"Glad to see you're your old self. May I use the 'Stang again today?" I asked in my sweetest tone of voice.

Blair rubbed her swollen eyes. "I don't know. I'm still sore at you about losing my horse." Her lacquered nails made a clicking sound against the Coke can as she reached for it. "To tell the truth, though, I'm a little scared to be here by myself." She bent her knees up to her chest and encircled them with her arms and took a swig of soda.

"So, here's an idea," I said. "Let me use the car and I'll take you with me." I wasn't anxious to have her interfere with me and Billy, but it didn't look like I had a choice. "Nothing bad will happen if we're together. Hurry up and eat," I said.

"Where are we going?" she asked.

"I'm going to confront Billy," I said. "Maybe you're right and he didn't kill Mandy, but he knows something. I want to know what." I didn't tell her about the break-in and attempt on my life. I didn't want her looking over her shoulder every five seconds. "First we'll try the parsonage, then if he's not there we'll head out to Hannibal Lake."

Watching Blair eat her breakfast made my stomach grumble and I realized that I hadn't eaten breakfast. A craving for a Mama Caldoni cannoli hit me, and hit me hard. If today was the day I got killed by Toni, the calories weren't going to hurt. "Get your clothes on," I said to Blair. "We're going to Mama Caldoni's for cannolis first."

"Super. Dessert for breakfast. That's definitely an idea that I can get behind." Blair reached across me and grabbed her robe off a nail. "I'll shower and be ready in ten."

"I'll be waiting in the car," I said.

Twenty minutes later, Blair slid behind the wheel in black spandex pants and a black polka dot sports bra showing plenty of cleavage, covered by a gauzy little black blouse, and strappy black wedgies.

I gave her the once-over. "Auditioning for a part in *Grease*?"

She gave me a haughty look. "There's nothing wrong with the way I'm dressed."

I wanted to make Billy talk, but it appeared she wanted to render him speechless. On the drive into town, Blair busied herself flipping radio channels, smacking her gum and pulling her hair into some semblance of order by securing it into a ponytail with a tight scrunchy. Seeming in a better mood, she waved at a couple merchants on Main Street who were beginning to open their stores and roll out displays onto the sidewalk. A farmers market was being held in the town square and old trucks had their tailgates lowered to display leafy greens, early tomatoes, potatoes and deep purple eggplants.

The 'Stang's tires thudded along the city's weathered brick streets. Blair slowed the car to a crawl and pulled into a parking space in front of Mama Caldoni's. Mama and Papa Caldoni had opened their diner featuring her meatloaf in the Seventies and hadn't changed the menu since. Mostly it was good solid truck stop food, except for the Italian cannoli, a hard, round pastry shell stuffed with a magical cream cheese mixture and bits of dried fruit and chocolate chips, rolled in powdered sugar.

A bell on the door jangled as we pushed it open. Old-timers at the soda fountain paused to look up from plates brimming with eggs and biscuits and white gravy. Samantha Peet sat at the counter enjoying a fruit cup. I gave her a shy smile and we made our way to the back booth. "If we have to go all the way out to Billy's cabin, remind me to get gas," Blair said to me, ignoring the stares.

The restaurant hadn't changed since I was a kid. Worn black-and-white squares of linoleum showed scorch marks from years of cigarettes being smashed underfoot. Red plastic seats, now cracked with little pouches of white batting showing through, perched atop silver stools by the soda fountain. We slid into a booth separated by dark paneled partitions from the booths on either side of it, in front of a smoky plate glass window. My fingertips found various hardened lumps of gum left under the chrome table rim through the years as I grabbed ahold to pull myself in.

"Same old same old," I said.

"Without a doubt," said Blair. "But they still have the best burgers in town."

An over-the-hill waitress in a pink uniform and saddle shoes brought some water and took our order. Blair dropped a quarter into the old table jukebox. "You make the selection," she said.

As I looked at the jukebox, the bell over the door jangled again and I looked up. A guy in low hung skater jeans and a black Megadeth T-shirt approached our table. His head, a shiny bald dome, sported a silver stud pushed though the bottom lip, and two through each eyebrow. I knew this guy. He was older, more muscular now, but the same guy I had seen years ago chucking chicken parts to alligators at Jerry's House of Reptiles, a tourist trap out on the interstate. I punched in "Bat Out of Hell" on the juke. Nothing like Meatloaf and a cannoli to start the day.

Blair took a sharp breath when she turned and saw the Megadeth guy.

"Hello ladies," he said in a deep, somehow familiar, voice as he schlepped to our table. "Want to deal?"

He stood at the end of our booth, smelling up the atmosphere with BO. "What deal?" I asked.

"It's a simple deal, really." He leaned over the table and whispered. "We get Mandy and you two get to keep on living."

"Hector, you're such an idiot," said Blair. "Next time you try to skewer one of my pet goats, I'll, I'll..."

Hector stuck a toothpick out that he'd been hiding in his mouth. He grabbed it between two dirty fingernails and poked Blair in the arm with it. She jumped. He looked around to make sure no one was listening and turned to me. "Let's just say I represent a group of interested parties who happen to believe you know where Mandy is."

"I have no idea where Mandy is," I lied.

"We wouldn't turn her over to a bunch of devil worshippers, even if we knew," added Blair.

He leaned toward me. "Don't worry. We won't hurt her."

"Liar. I know you want to kill her baby," I said.

He leaned into the booth so that no one could see and pinched the soft meat of my underarm.

I jerked away. "Quit it, asshole," I said, rubbing it.

"So you're smart enough to have figured out what we want. Well, maybe you're smart enough to understand this. Mandy must be consecrated in blood on the full moon." He stared at me through creepy gold contacts that elongated his pupils like a cat's. "This is the most important thing we've ever done. Unlimited power with Father Satan will be ours."

I waited for him to bellow out a mad laugh like in a Frankenstein movie. He didn't.

He reached for my arm again and I jerked away in time. He sneered and shoved in to sit down beside Blair and put his arm around her. "You know that snow globe you had by your bed? I have it now." Blair and I looked at each other. "Think about it," he said, giving her shoulder a squeeze. He turned toward me. "You should really get an exterminator for those bats."

"What is he talking about?" Blair asked me.

The waitress sashayed over with our cannoli and a big smile. She placed one in front of Blair and then put mine on the table. "Bon appetit," she said, as she swirled away to pour coffee for other patrons. Blair and I pushed away our plates at practically the same moment. "Not hungry," I said.

Hector pulled my plate over and took a bite of the cannoli, leaving powdered sugar on his upper lip. "I didn't get to treat you like you deserve, but there will be other nights. At least I got something for my trouble. Some cash and some fun."

Sounding braver than I felt, I said, "You're not as scary as you think, Satan Boy. Get lost."

He took something out of his pocket and handed it to Blair.

"Not scared, huh. Well, I'll bet you want to see this bad boy again. Too bad. I didn't want to use him for the deal, because I planned on keeping him. You give us Mandy, you get him back."

Blair choked on some water she'd been drinking and handed the picture to me. It was a photo of Hector in full satanic getup, standing next to Darkwater.

My knee-jerk reaction was so swift, it happened before I could stop myself. Hector groaned, slumped forward, and held his crotch where my right foot had landed in the middle of his junk with a righteous kick from under the table. Blair and I hurried out, leaving Hector the Satan Boy with our cannoli and the tab.

"You may regret that someday," Blair said to me as we made the bell on the door jangle again.

"I'm already sorry," I said. "I hope they don't hurt Darkwater. Let's go find Billy."

Chapter Nineteen

Blair and I positioned ourselves in the 'Stang in a hurry. I clicked my seat belt shut as fast as I could. "To think that creep was in my bedroom!" said Blair as she pulled out of the parking space. "I'm afraid. Aren't you?"

I thought about it for a minute. "I'm sick of being afraid," I said. "Those thugs aren't going to rule my life. Billy and I are having it out today."

Blair pushed her finger into my chest. "You're wrong about Billy," she said.

"Does the truth have to come up and bite you in the ass?" I asked her. "Billy was leading that pack of hyenas the night I rescued you."

"How can you be so sure? You didn't see his face, did you?"

"Whoever I saw was wearing snakeskin boots like Billy's. Whoever I saw was the same height as Billy. He walked like Billy. I figure if it walks like a duck and quacks like a duck, it's probably Billy."

"Don't be ridiculous. Boots like that are sold in every shoe store in South Dakota." Blair pushed the button to put the top down on the convertible.

"Just because you've licked his tonsils doesn't mean you know a guy," I said.

Blair and I drove in silence to the Chance home.

It looked like Billy's folks had made some attempt to put their individual stamp on the parsonage, a small cottage next to the church. Tulip shapes were cut into the short wooden fence around the yard. Window shutters, painted yellow and blue, had heart shapes carved into them. Some kind of creeping vine had attached itself to the gingerbread-colored walls. Very Hansel and Gretel.

Tidy as a marine's bed, the yard was a thick carpet of green, and here and there were topiary straight out of Edward Scissorhands. Ardis Chance, in broad-brimmed straw hat and gardeners gloves, clipped a hedge that resembled a poodle. Disney could use her, I thought as I studied the bizarre little house.

"Hello, Reverend," Blair called out, interrupting my thoughts. "Is Billy home?"

Ardis looked up and smiled when she saw Blair but her smile faltered when I leaned forward in the seat and waved. She took a handkerchief from her jeans pocket and stroked her forehead. "Good morning, girls. No, I'm not sure where Billy's gotten himself off to. He said something about moving his stuff into the cabin at Hannibal Lake. Anything I can do to help you?"

"That's okay. We'll catch up with him later," said Blair.

I put my hand over Blair's, which was resting on the gearshift. "Wait a second," I said.

I turned away from Ardis and picked a drawstring pouch of protective power stones out of my purse. I shook the stones out, and discreetly placed the upside down black cross from Mandy's crucifix in it, along with the pocket-sized Luciferian Primer book I had picked up at Billy's cabin. I double-knotted the pouch closed, and handed it to Ardis. I figured if I didn't catch up to Billy, he would be sure to come looking for me once he saw what was in the pouch. "In case we don't catch him, give him this," I said.

"What's this?" Ardis asked as I handed her the pouch.

"Just something of Billy's that he left at the Bonnie B."

Ardis slid the pouch into her pocket. "I'll see he gets it. How's your aunt and Ruby doing?"

"She and Ruby should get out on bail today," I said.

"At least the wedding ceremony was out of the way before all that nasty business," said Ardis as she commenced clipping the hedge.

"Yes, fortunate," I said. "And Reverend, I did like the ceremony. You said some beautiful and insightful things about the sanctity of marriage." I figured it wouldn't hurt to spread it on thick with her.

She looked surprised. "Why, thank you, River. I meant every word. Young people today take marriage much too lightly."

"Perhaps," I said. "I hear Billy is engaged to Mandy." The devil must've made me say that.

Her clippers made a loud chop as they closed around a branch. "Wherever did you hear that piece of nonsense? Marriage requires informed consent. Mandy is not a person who can think about the consequences of her decisions. She would never be one my Billy would marry. Give my best to Colin. Tell him I'll be praying for them." She adjusted her straw hat and dismissed us sharply, turning her back to us.

We pulled away. "I don't think she's too thrilled with you," said Blair. "What say we put some miles between her and us before she throws rocks. Let's go out to the Rez and see the baby. You can show me the way."

I studied her. "For someone who didn't want this baby around, you sure are anxious to see him again."

A smile tugged at the corners of her mouth. "No big deal. I just want to see how the little guy's doing."

And maybe Toni will be there and I can beat the shit out of her I thought.

"Manage to stay under the speed limit, okay?" I said.

She laughed. "We've broken so many laws already. What's a traffic violation?" She pushed down the accelerator and morphed into Danica Patrick.

Thankfully, we didn't encounter any cops on the way to the Rez. Blair never said a word. I guess she was concentrating on how to keep the car on the road at one hundred twenty mph. Finally, she braked hard to a stop in front of John's farmhouse, barely missing Bruce where he sat on the rock fence picking his nose. That little rascal of Madeline's was always in the wrong place at the wrong time, and this time it very nearly got him killed. My heart was beating so fast I flew out of the car like an escaped prisoner and took deep breaths.

Bruce sprang off the fence, eyes big as stop signs, and ran to the porch bawling. I opened my mouth to unload on Blair, but I could see she was about to burst into tears. I put my hand on her arm. "He's okay, Blair. No harm done. Don't cry."

"It's not just Bruce. It's this whole mess," she wailed.

"C'mon. We'll get through this thing together," I said.

"Will we? It's not just that we've broken I don't know how many laws. It's more than that. It's…oh, I don't know… I've always thought I knew what I wanted." Her eyes searched my face like she expected me to guess what that was. I must have looked clueless.

She grunted in exasperation and stretched her hands out, palms up, fingers splayed. "To get the hell out of here and go to New York! But now, with the baby, I don't…it's just weird. I never thought I would feel sorry for your sister. But when I looked at that baby, and I thought about Mandy never being able to see her own son, it made me…so angry. Whoever did that to her has got to be punished!"

I was surprised at her deep feeling. "They will. I promise." I patted her shoulder. "C'mon. Let's go in." I said.

"Hey little guy," I said as we passed Bruce peeking at us from around the corner of the house. His face and naked chest were covered in something sticky. I noticed bees bouncing off a busted cantaloupe that lay splayed open in the yard. "Good melon?" I asked. He looked at me with a sulky stare. I knocked on the door and John pushed open the screen door. He wore only jeans, and a leather cord with a totem pouch attached around his neck. Bruce jumped back when he caught sight of John.

"Hi, John. Bruce is a little upset with us," I said.

"He stays upset, that one. Come on in," he said, stepping aside for us to enter. "The two babies are taking a lot of his mother's attention. She seems to always have one or the other up at her tits. I'm trying to make up for it by spending time with Bruce, giving him treats, but I think he's had enough of me. I got a clue when he launched that melon at me." He grinned. "If you want to see my grandson, Madeline has the babies back there." He motioned to the bedroom past an oil painting of two wolves baying at a harvest moon. It was signed by Toni.

"Have you seen Toni around?" I asked him.

"She was here this morning. Took off on one of the horses. Haven't seen her since."

Madeline smiled at us as we entered the bedroom, but looked weary. She had Mandy's baby cuddled to her breast. He was wrapped tight in a receiving blanket like a mini human burrito. His fists were tucked next to his fat cheeks as he suckled. Fine black hair swept into a tuft on the top of his head.

Blair, who had been so angry, now had a dumbstruck puppy-love look on her face. "Oh, he's so cute," she said and proceeded to make kootchie-coo sounds as she cupped his tiny foot in her hand.

"You want to burp him?" asked Madeline. "I could sure use the help."

Blair gingerly accepted the small bundle and put him over her shoulder. Madeline handed her a cloth diaper as she picked up her own infant and put him to her other breast. Blair placed the diaper under her brother's chin, and then walked the room patting his back and bobbing slightly. After a few back pats, the baby gave a satisfying belch.

I turned to Madeline. "Thanks for taking care of Mandy's baby," I said.

"I'm glad to help. John's been so good to me."

I sat down on the bed by her. "I was sorry to hear about your husband. John told me he was killed in Iraq."

She pushed her black-rimmed glasses up on her nose. "Thank you. It was hard. Paul had been in Iraq two years when it happened. He got to come home during his tour for a couple months on leave, just long enough to get me pregnant and take off again. You know, Paul and I never made our marriage official, so the government didn't give me any insurance or anything for him. It went to his folks, I guess. They don't want anything to do with me or the children. I probably would've starved without John."

"He seems to like your kids," I said, affected by her story.

She took off her glasses and rubbed the bridge of her nose. "What will happen to him?" She nodded toward Blair and the sleeping infant. "I wouldn't mind making a home for him, if that's what John wants. It would be like having twins."

"I don't know."

"Blair sure seems taken with the baby," she said.

"Yeah, that's something I never thought I'd see," I said. "I didn't think Blair cared about anybody but herself."

"Babies have a way of making a person change priorities," Madeline offered.

"Yep," I said and stood up. "Time to get going. C'mon," I called to Blair.

Blair leaned over the crib and gave the sleeping infant a kiss as she laid him down. "Thanks for taking care of my little brother," she said.

Madeline smiled, acknowledging her with a nod.

Chapter Twenty

"What in the world?" Billy glared at me when he opened his cabin door and saw me standing there. When he saw Blair coming up behind me, his face softened. He motioned us in. "So what are you girls up to today?" He walked to the counter and picked up a side of bacon, cutting it into thick slices with a sharp knife. He arranged them in a pan and put them on a burner. "Bacon, lettuce and tomato for brunch. Want one, Blair? I'd ask River if she wants one, but vampires only eat blood. Right, River?" He laughed at his own stupid joke as he sliced a tomato.

"Duh hah, duh hah. Funny guy." I tried to think how to approach Billy with my questions as Blair and Billy blathered on about some vampire movie they'd both seen as bacon grease popped and danced in the pan. "Billy, I'm not here to socialize," I finally said. I put my hands on my hips. "I want you to know I'm on to you."

He looked at me like I was a booger on the end of his finger.

He slid the hot bacon onto a paper towel. "What is it you think you know?"

Blair spoke up. "Billy, you know I care about you," she said. "I don't believe what River believes."

"What are you two talking about?" he asked as he built his sandwich, sat down at the table and took a bite.

I tried to use my sixth sense to form a bubble above his head that would reveal his thoughts. Nothing. Evidently it only worked with animals.

I hadn't meant to tell anyone, least of all the sheriff's son, about Mandy's death, but I decided to take a chance. Billy's reaction to the news would tell me if he was lying or not. If he was lying, I'd pummel him on the spot and make him tell me about the cult and the attempt on my life and Toni's involvement. If he wasn't lying and truly loved Mandy, as he professed, I'd know that, too. He had a right to know about her death.

So, I just came out with it. "We found Mandy on Old Mill Road Friday night," I said. "Someone ran over her."

Billy wiped his mouth, balled up the napkin and threw it at me. "That ain't funny, River."

"It's true. She's dead," said Blair. "But, the baby is fine."

The shock on his face looked real. The low moan that seemed to come right up from his gut certainly sounded sincere. The plate hit the floor as Billy leaned forward, put his head on the table and clutched his stomach. Then he jumped up, ran to the sink, and threw up.

I don't know the reaction I expected, but this wasn't it. Blair rushed to him and gently placed her arms around his shoulders as he leaned into the sink. She gave me a helpless look as she handed him a towel. He composed himself and wiped his mouth, then turned to me, holding onto Blair. "How? Did the police catch who did it?"

"No," I said. Part of me felt sorry for him and the other part wondered if he was a pretty good actor.

"I just *knew* something bad had happened to her," he said as he took a few sips of water. "I just knew it. She was with me when we pulled into the Gas Up and Go. She was talking crazy about selling the baby when it came. She thought I'd be happy.

Said I wouldn't be 'bothered' by the baby anymore."

He put down the glass. "I tried to tell her it's illegal to sell a baby, that I wanted the baby, but she didn't understand. We got into a big argument and I just ended up making her mad. When I got back from paying for the gas, she wasn't in the truck. I couldn't find her anywhere. The only thing I can think is for her to disappear that fast she must've gotten into a car with someone."

"You're a rotten liar," I said, thinking I had caught him. "I saw Mandy in this very cabin, your cabin, the night she died. Are you trying to make me believe she wasn't here with you? You're lying just like you lied about not having a gun and forcing my mother to her death."

Billy looked stricken. "*Enough*," he shouted. Anger flashed in his eyes. "I never, never meant to hurt your mother. And I swear I didn't see Mandy after the gas station. Why was she here at the cabin? Had she come looking for me?" He pulled his hand through his hair. "Well, that makes no sense. She knew I was staying with my folks. Samantha was staying out here and Mandy knew that. Why would she come here?"

"Samantha Peet stayed here?" I asked in surprise.

"Yeah, she's somewhere around here now, too. I saw her in her car not far from here. She told me she was looking for a Palm Pilot that fell out of her pack when she was hiking around the lake."

Blair looked at her shoes. "I guess you really loved Mandy, huh?"

"Yes. I love her. Her and the baby."

"Did she tell you the baby was Colin's?" I asked.

His face showed no surprise at the question. "Not in so many words," he said. "But, I knew. I asked her the right questions. Before she knew she was pregnant, she told me she could feel something moving inside her. I put my hand on her belly and I felt the baby move. I asked her if she'd 'played the game' with anyone. That's what she called having sex."

"And you know that how?" asked Blair.

"Not how you think," he said. "Once she heard some of the guys kidding me about being a player. When she asked me what a player was, I was straight with her. I told her that it meant the guys thought I rubbed tushies with girls. She said she knew that game. That it was a game she'd played only with Colin."

"What about the cult?" Blair asked. "Are you part of that? River is sure she saw you at a coven meeting."

"I'm not part of the cult. I just pretended to be so I could find out who is involved," Billy said. "You know, to help Colin. He's been going nuts about his cattle and afraid the Satanists would spook his guests when the ranch opens in the fall. The night you two caused such a ruckus at the coven meeting was the first time I talked Toni into letting me come."

"Toni?" I said.

The window shattered. My mind registered the blast of a gun. Shards of glass scattered everywhere. I dove behind a chair as Billy slumped forward, grabbing his arm. Blair clutched her stomach and dropped to the floor. The door flew open and Ardis stood there glaring down at me, a shotgun barrel pointed at my nose. Her eyes were hard and beady.

Then she saw Billy. "You stupid boy…" were the only words she spoke. She dropped the gun and slumped to her knees in a faint. I heard Billy slide to the floor two heartbeats later.

Rational thought eluded me. I could almost feel the adrenaline slamming into my muscles, forcing my legs to get me up. Raw rage propelled me across the room. I kicked the rifle across the floor and slapped Ardis hard on the cheek. Her eyelids fluttered. I could see Blair out of the corner of my eye, unconscious with blood seeping out of her middle.

"Mom!" said Billy as he clamped his hand over his shoulder. "What the hell…"

"Did I kill him?" Ardis asked as she sputtered back to consciousness. Tears rolled down her cheeks as she looked up at me. "Did I kill my wayward son?" She reached toward Billy.

"Yes," said Billy. "You killed me with my own goddamned shotgun."

"Sit still," I said, bowling her over with my foot and straddling her to keep her stationary. "Billy, can you make it to your phone?"

"Get off me," she yelled as she flailed at me with her arms.

"Billy's been hurt!"

"I know," I said. "*You* shot him! You're not getting another crack at him while he's down." I managed to pin her arms as Billy got up and staggered toward the phone.

"I would never intentionally hurt my son," she said. "Pain for the sake of discipline, yes. But not this. This was an accident. It's all your fault! The things you left in that pouch…You said they were his. I came here to question him and now look what happened."

"Those things were for his eyes only," I said. "Besides, I'd say bringing a gun and putting those shot pellets in his arm is more of a statement than a question."

"I didn't mean to do that! I was shooting at you! When I pulled up, you jumped me from behind."

"What other planets have you been visiting today, Ardis?" I said.

"Don't pretend it wasn't you. You choked me unconscious and dragged me to that shed out back with that awful stuff you have in there. Devil things. Black candles, awful books, robes." She motioned to the red marks on her neck. "See what she did, son?"

"It wasn't me," I said.

"Oh, yes it was, you Jezebel." She reached to Billy again. "I couldn't let her get away with that, son. So I got your gun from your truck and loaded it with ammo I found in the glove compartment. Her I meant to end, but not you. Now get off me, you Daughter of Satan!"

"Daughter of…? Do you want me to strangle you for real?"

"Daughter of Satan! Daughter of Satan!" she yelled.

I willed myself to be calm and stayed firmly planted across her lap. I tightened my hold around her wrists. "Think about it. Would I join any club that would have Billy as a member?"

"Don't try to deny it, you floozie. When I saw that perverted crucifix you left for Billy, I knew it was from the devil just like the one I saw on that retarded girl. Trying to recruit him for that awful cult was your undoing." She spat at me. "Look at the trouble you've caused." She twisted under me.

"You saw Mandy wearing the crucifix?" I asked. "When?"

Billy suddenly blanched even whiter and stopped before picking up the phone.

"I, I don't remember," said Ardis, mumbling her words.

"You saw it the night she died, didn't you? That was the only time she wore it," I accused.

"No. I don't... Get off me!" The look on Ardis's face told me I was onto something.

"You were drinking, weren't you, Mom?" Billy said, though teeth clenched in pain. "You always drink on Friday night when Dad's on late patrol. You hit Mandy, didn't you? And left her for dead. Her and the baby."

"Yes, I did!" she shouted at him. "You should be glad I did! It was God's gift to me to catch her out like that. I couldn't let you marry that girl. What future would you have had with her? None!"

Ardis was getting pretty worked up and harder to hold down. "Jesus, Billy, punch in nine-one-one for those goddamned medics," I wailed.

Suddenly Ardis seemed renewed. She bucked under me. "Do not use the name of our Lord in vain," she shouted as she rolled and tumbled me off. On my knees, I made a grab for her as she headed to the door.

Enraged, she turned on me, grabbing my hair with one hand and slapping me hard with the other one. I put my fist into her thigh. She let go of my hair, but her kick made contact with my gut.

I looked up to see Samantha in the doorway. "Help," I yelled and rolled into a fetal position. Samantha flew in, pummeling Ardis. Ardis broke away and ran to her car. I saw her personalized license place *REVRUND* fade into the dust.

I picked myself up. "Shit, shit, shit," I said.

Billy didn't speak. He closed his eyes, then lost consciousness.

My body was all out of moves and my brain went into shutdown mode. It barely registered when Samantha snapped on rubber gloves and picked up the shotgun.

Chapter Twenty-one

"Cleopatra, I presume," I said.

I fingered what I was sure was a beefy black eye in the making. What a puke I am, I thought. I wasn't even able to best a senior citizen. I collected myself and stood up. I rubbed my arms where the reverend's nicely manicured nails had sliced me. I was sore, but everything felt like it was in the right place.

"You know, River, you are truly pissing me off," Samantha said.

"Yeah, and I'm really in love with you, too," I said as I rubbed my jaw.

She circled me as she walked toward the phone and hung it up. "You're such a little bitch. A troublemaker. Just like your mother."

I have to admit that one threw me for a loop. "Wha?" I said.

"Oh yes. Your mother. Quite the hussy. Tried to take my man. My man," she emphasized.

"What man?" I asked.

"Buster."

"You're crazy," I said. "She'd never have loved anyone like Buster." Then I thought of how she had loved John, who was totally wrong for her, and wondered.

"I learned about their little fling the night of the parent-teacher conference. Billy peeked in the window, saw them kissing. He didn't know what to do. If he'd interrupted, he felt sure Buster would hit him. So he came and got me." Samantha's face flushed. "Buster was kissing her the way he'd kissed me. Hot. Passionate. The fucker."

She waved the shotgun. "I'd seen you go down to the basement earlier. I told Billy that if he went down there and made you scream, Briana and Buster would stop and come to see what was wrong with you. That boy was so sure his mother would kill Buster if she caught him with another woman he'd have done anything to make them stop. Later, he made me laugh when he told me you wouldn't yell when he pushed you, so he showed you his penis and then you screamed."

I bit my lip to make sure this was real and not a nightmare. "Mom was not in love with Buster," I said, hoping it was true. "Besides, he was and is a married man, Samantha. You had no right to even be jealous." I don't know what made me say that. I made a mental note to myself not to argue with a crazy person who has a gun trained on me.

Samantha blinked several times at that obviously foreign thought and tried to make me see her point of view. "He was mine. I knew Ardis wasn't meeting his needs. She confided that to me herself. As long as she wasn't having sex with him and I was, I was his real wife. But Briana was a different matter. She had to die."

"What do you mean?" My brain itched where a new thought was forming. "You didn't kill my mother. Billy did."

"Don't be stupid. That little dink could hardly point his penis at the toilet and pee, much less murder someone. Of course it didn't turn out the way I planned either, for that matter. I had meant to shoot that whore right between the eyes during the field trip."

"That wasn't much of a plan," I said. "You'd have spent your life in prison."

"Not if I was secretive enough. Buster would have fixed things for me. He always fixed things. Like he fixed it when I set Clive's house on fire. I never really liked that Clive. When he tried to blackmail Buster, I felt a moral responsibility to help Buster out." Again she waved the gun. "But, anyhow, where was I? Oh, yes, I was about to shoot Briana when some stupid kid interrupted me, so I discreetly slid the gun into Billy's pocket as he stood next to me. Then, before I could stop him, he ran off. I was about to yell at him to get away from the cliff, when I got an idea. I knew the ground was muddy and slick up there. I told Briana that I'd seen Billy with a gun and he was suicidal. By this time, Billy had discovered it and took it out of his pocket. Briana was never afraid of anything. Off she went, marching right up to Billy. She slipped as she tried to get the gun. End of Briana."

I willed myself not to walk over to Samantha and slam her smug mug into the wall. The shotgun she held went a long way toward me keeping my resolve.

"So, what do you want? To kill me, too? Will Buster cover for you again? Bodies are beginning to stack up around you like pancakes, Samantha. I would think that would be a real deterrent to a sound relationship."

"As I said, you're pissing me off. I was listening from outside. I heard you say Mandy was dead. Where is that goddamned baby? I've already promised him to a family. I need that fifty-thousand dollars."

"You mean you sell babies? You don't sacrifice them?"

"Swift on the uptake, aren't you. No, I don't sacrifice them. So far, me and my lawyer buddy have placed three." She sounded proud of the fact. "The stupid bozos in the cult thought I sacrificed them. They kidnap the babies for me and I give them a show. I do some sleight of hand with a doll and animal parts then I say a few words over it all and eventually throw it into a fire. They're always so stoned, they can't tell the difference. Good drugs make good minions. Now, show-and-tell is over. Tell me where that baby is and die fast. Don't, and die slow and hard."

My heart nearly stopped when I saw Toni through the open cabin door sneaking up behind Samantha. Samantha must've seen something in my face, because she turned slightly toward the door. In what seemed like slow motion, I saw Toni bend over and pick up a baseball-sized rock. I saw her right leg drop back as she stepped into the winning form that must've won her the pitching trophy she told me about when we first met. I saw her step into the throw with her left foot and extend her right arm forward. I saw the release. Saw the rock travel across the expanse. I dove for cover.

The shotgun discharged just as the rock knocked it from Samantha's hand. "You stupid fool!" screamed Samantha as she ran for the gun. Toni burst through the door and knocked Samantha sideways, kicking the shotgun under the table. Samantha picked up the bacon knife off the counter and lashed at Toni, slicing her leg, causing her to stumble. Then she ran at me with the knife, her eyes wild and her lips pulled back.

I dropped and rolled onto my back as she lunged at me. I caught her arms, pushing my foot into her stomach and somersaulted her over the top of me, a little trick I learned from my foster brothers. She dropped the knife and sprawled on the floor a few feet away, then righted herself and ran for the door. I ran after her.

She jumped in the 'Stang, and we fought like girls as she turned the key in the ignition, me slapping at her hands and trying to pull her from the driver's seat and her slapping my hands back. She opened the door against me with a mighty hit, sending me sprawling back on the ground on my ass. The engine did a continuous grind. My heart leapt with joy as I realized I'd forgotten to remind Blair to get gas. The car wouldn't start.

The horse Toni had been riding bareback was standing by a tree and Samantha ran for it, grabbing the reins and swinging her leg over, kicking him hard. The horse, confused at the urgent jerking of the reins while being kicked, did a little backward dance. I puckered my lips into a whistle for him to stop, but my lip was split from the fight, and I couldn't get it out.

I closed my eyes and sent the horse a thought picture of

him rearing up. When I opened them, I saw his front feet come up, churning the air. Samantha grabbed for his neck in a futile attempt to hold on. Unable to get a grip, she slid off his sleek back, landing between his dancing feet and hitting the ground hard. I held my breath as the horse stumbled and his muscular body fell backward.

After that, the only part of Samantha Peet left to be seen under a ton of horse was her hand, her fingers limp and white.

Chapter Twenty-two

"I thought FBI agents carried guns," I said as Toni and I lay on the roof, naked together on a blanket, soaking up rays. I felt safe. Who was going to see us on the roof?

"I was undercover, River. I'd stand out a little if I packed heat. Besides, I was out for a leisurely horseback ride. I didn't know I'd be stumbling into Dodge City at high noon."

I gently traced the fresh stitches on Toni's thigh with my finger. "You could have let me know who you really were. I wouldn't have told anyone. It was scary when I thought you and Hector were going to kill me. Was everything you said to me a lie?"

"Some of it was lies, yes. But the kind of lies I tell are to keep people like Samantha from succeeding. And no, I couldn't tell you. Secrecy is key in an investigation like this. Samantha and her lawyer friend in Memphis will spend a long time in jail because they didn't know who I was. Hence, the term 'undercover.' Besides, I was never going to let Hector hurt you. I planned to push him off the roof if I had to."

"Hence? How old are you, anyway?"

"Twenty-four."

I was surprised. "That's a little young to be an agent, isn't it?"

"I suppose," said Toni. "I graduated high school at seventeen, did college in four. You know how it is. Someone you know knows someone who needs to fill a minority slot and fast-tracks your application to the academy."

I sat up and rubbed baby oil on my legs and arms. "Your body's not too bad for an old chick," I said. "What part of all those lies you told me was true?"

"Charley really is my grandfather. Poor John must've been in quite a quandary, not wanting to let his old friend down when Charley asked for him to help me, but not wanting an FBI agent in his house, either."

"Man, he does hate the Bureau," I said. She took the oil from me. I turned over and she rubbed it on my back. "That part about liking you, that was true," Toni piped up. "I'm really, deeply, in like with you." She reached around and gently rubbed her hand over my nipple. "Could turn into love someday, given time and your absolutely unwavering devotion to me."

"Oh, you are shameless tempting me with that carrot on a stick routine," I said. "You could fall in love with me yes, but more likely, you'll be on your way to yet another exciting assignment somewhere with some international babe spy."

I smiled and turned over and embraced her, both of us shiny with baby oil and slipping against each other like eels. "But I do forgive you. If you hadn't been FBI and been there to explain what I did to Mandy, I'd probably be in jail for attempted kidnapping or murder."

Toni hunched her shoulders in a no big deal way. "Autopsy reports were inconclusive, but I know what you did was necessary, River. There was no way to save Mandy, and you saved the baby. That's what I put in my report. You know, River, it blows my mind when I think about how badly this could have turned out for you."

"Wakan Tanka took care of it, just like John said He would. Samantha will never walk again or be free, if she recovers. And Buster's under investigation for any role he may have had in Clive's death."

"Let's not forget crazy Ardis," she said. "Oh, did I tell you? They picked her up in Nebraska."

"And Hector?"

"He's still out there somewhere. Don't worry. You can't hide for long from the long arm of the law," she said as she slid her hand down and cupped my bun and squeezed. "It'll take a little time, but we'll quash the whole nasty baby-selling and drug-running scheme and everyone connected to it."

"Quash? No, really. How old are you?" I asked.

"Twenty-six."

"Imagine." I pinched her butt. "And no visible cellulite anywhere."

"Thank goodness Billy and Blair will be okay," she said. "I think your aunt's legal troubles are over. Colin told me that the Buttrams called this morning from Arizona to congratulate him on his marriage. They'd heard about the wedding from one of their relatives in Pell Mell. When Colin told them about Ruby and Angela being in trouble, Mr. Buttram remembered a handwritten letter they'd gotten from Birdie, tucked in a Bible she'd given them on the day they left. Birdie thanked them for their service and for hiding the Caitlen necklace for safekeeping in the wall until she could get it to Aunt Angela. I think when Judge Koop sees that letter, authenticated by a writing expert, he'll dismiss the case. After all, you can't steal what you already own."

I was about to hip, holler and hooray when the noise of a car pulling in the drive underneath us distracted us both. John's old pink Cadillac with a beat-up horse trailer were pulling under the cottonwood tree by the corral. John got out and backed Darkwater out of the trailer, cooing gently as he pushed on the horse's flanks to back him down the ramp.

The kitchen door quivered under Colin's thrust as he made his way out of it and strode toward John. His movements were fluid, filled with purpose, his head up. His hands had closed into tight fists. He looked like a prizefighter making his way to the ring. Toni and I looked at each other, our eyebrows raised in speculation.

"Colin," John acknowledged him curtly as he approached.

"John," returned Colin. "Seems you got my horse there. What you doing with my horse?" His square jaw raised up a hitch.

John's face showed no emotion as he swished at a fly on the horse's back. "I found him down by Nell's Creek. Someone had rigged a paddock under the trees. Seemed like they were treating him okay. Had plenty of grain and water."

Colin's face relaxed slightly. He rubbed his hand over the horse's back, sliding his hands down Darkwater's legs and picking up his feet. He checked each one, dropping each with a thud. Then he reached up and pulled back the horse's lips, examining his mouth thoroughly.

"Doesn't look like he was drugged," he said, rubbing his hands over the horse's underbelly. "Seems okay. There's a reward." The words were said slowly and with effort. "Come on in. I'll write you a check."

John walked Darkwater the short distance to the corral and led him in. "Come on in, you say? You'll write me a check? Don't you really want to hit me instead? Don't you want to get in your truck and try to run me down again?" John closed the corral gate and leaned his gangly frame against a fence post.

Colin clenched and unclenched his fists. "Of course, I'd like to hit you. But, it won't bring Bonnie back, will it? I don't think there'd be much point in it, do you?"

"It might make us both feel better."

"Just take the money and go," Colin said, as he turned toward the house.

"I'm here to see if things can be better between us now," said John. "There's much at stake."

Colin hesitated. "I don't think so," he said, then continued walking.

"I know things would've been different if I had listened to you years ago," John persisted. "I shouldn't have talked to Bonnie when you said to stop. But I wanted to make her understand. Our own young people seemed to be forgetting our way of life, our traditions. Bonnie wanted to know about the Red Road, and I just kept talking to her, despite your warnings to leave her alone. I truly regret that. Only Wakan Tanka knows why Bonnie came out to the ranch that day instead of going on to the hospital. I swear, I never told her to do that."

Colin shrugged. "I've figured that one out. She did it because she trusted you more than she ever trusted me."

"There was never anything between me and Bonnie," said John. "If that's what you're getting at."

"Don't flatter yourself. I know Bonnie loved me. What I mean is I didn't listen to her. I only tried to control her. I tried to tell her how to act, even how to think."

"You thought you were protecting her. We all try to protect those we love," said John. "Sometimes we think controlling them is the best way to do that."

Colin looked at John with such unblinking focus that I wouldn't have been surprised to see electricity leap across the space. Finally, he said, "You and I will never be friends. But I've come to realize that what happened with Bonnie and the baby was as much my fault as yours. She never would have been talking to you, if she felt she could talk to me."

John extended his hand. "I know it took a lot for you to say that to me. You say we can't be friends. That's okay. Can we be men together? Nod to each other when we meet on the street? Maybe do some horse business?"

"We'll see about doing business," said Colin. "But, yes, we can be civil." He took John's hand and shook it. "You want the reward? It's yours."

"No," said John. "We need to talk further. I have something else that belongs to you." He walked to the Cadillac and pulled out the baby, tucked in a big plastic baby carry seat with a handle.

John brushed horsehair off his jeans with one hand as he carried the baby with the other and turned and walked toward the house. Colin, dumbfounded, followed. As we watched them walk into the house, I had my fingers crossed that Ruby would turn out to be the compassionate, forgiving person I thought she was.

"She'll love him on sight," said Toni, as if reading my thoughts. We scooted ourselves back onto our blanket, our little oasis. I thought about Billy as Toni and I were silent together, spooning, her arm draped over me.

I thought about how for years he'd carried the image of my mother's last moments. I saw in my mind what he must've seen. My mother slipping, flailing her arms. I realized now that I'd seen him reaching for her, gun in hand, unable to stop her from going over. He was just a child, and when she'd grabbed for him he'd been afraid, realizing that she'd pull him over, too. He'd stepped back. He faced each day with the guilt that he couldn't save her.

Another memory came to me. A memory of that night on the road so clear that it cut through the fog in my brain that had been separating what was imagined from what was real. I became aware, in that moment, laying on the roof with Toni, that the cut I'd made in Mandy had been the decisive one. The one that had killed her. The baby had called out to me on a primitive animal wavelength to save him, and I had unconsciously heard him. Like Billy, I'd have to live with the choice I had made.

"You're much too solemn, my girl," said Toni as she buried her neck in mine and hugged me tight. She rolled over on top of me and put her fingertips on my lips, outlining them softly with her touch.

My tears trickled down onto her hand. "I feel like I have a big gaping wound right here," I said as I guided her hand down between my breasts, where the warmth emanating from her palm felt like the sun thawing a block of ice.

"That wound will heal," she said. "You're strong, River. If you look deep inside yourself, you know it will. It will take time, but I can feel it right now, healing under my hand."

I knew she was right, and I kissed her deeply for reminding me of that, and lost myself in the wonder of her.